CAUGHT!

Lights off, I felt my way around the desk, peered out through the door, and slipped out, pulling it shut hard behind me. Ah! Whew.

Suddenly there was a whoosh of movement behind me, an arm clamped hard against my throat. My head jerked back. I tried to scream, to gasp, but bug-eyed, I found I couldn't even breathe.

A voice whispered roughly against my hair. "Listen, you. You get out of here and you mind your own business, you hear me?"

"An exciting horse racing mystery . . .
The villains are villainous
and the danger sometimes terrifying."
School Library Journal

RIDE A DARK HORSE

Lynn Hall

AN AVON FLARE BOOK

AVON BOOKS
A division of
The Hearst Corporation
105 Madison Avenue
New York, New York 10016

Copyright © 1987 by Lynn Hall
Published by arrangement with the author
Library of Congress Catalog Card Number: 87-12310
ISBN: 0-380-75370-7
RL: 6.1

Published in hardcover by William Morrow and Company, Inc.; for information address Permissions Department, William Morrow and Company, Inc., 105 Madison Avenue, New York, New York 10016.

First Avon Flare Printing: October 1988

AVON FLARE TRADEMARK REG. U.S. PAT. OFF. AND IN OTHER COUNTRIES, MARCA
REGISTRADA, HECHO EN U.S.A.

Printed in the U.S.A.

K-R 10 9 8 7 6 5 4 3 2

1

I was seventeen when my world blew up in my face. I wasn't ready to handle it. How could anyone ever be ready to lose the only person who loves her?

For three months after Pop died I moved around like a robot and only began to snap out of it the night I saw the lights above the breeding shed.

Pop died in February, but Mr. DeVrees said I could stay on in the apartment till May, when I'd have to move to the single girls' quarters so R.B. could have the apartment. R.B. was getting married and needed the extra room, although it was hard to imagine any girl being dumb enough or desperate enough to sign on for a life sentence with that creep. I'd been dodging his dirty hands since I was thirteen.

Tradition Farm was two thousand acres of prime bluegrass in southern Ohio with a view, on a clear day, across the Ohio River into Kentucky. All the buildings were limestone, from the main house to the tool sheds and gateposts. It cost seven thousand dollars a year just to keep the paddock fences painted. Luckily Mrs. Jewett, who owned us all, didn't have to sweat the minor bills like that one, not with Ambassador raking in three-hundred-thousand-dollar stud fees.

To understand the social structure at Tradition

Farm, picture a pyramid. Mrs. Jewett was the peak. Under her were a pair of guys, accountants or something, who handled the business end of her fortune, and Mr. DeVrees, who ran the stable and, in my private opinion, was bucking for promotion to Mr. Jewett's old job, husband and prince consort to the Jewett money. At least he seemed to follow Mrs. J. around more than necessary, and while I never saw him actually licking her boots, he did have the art of groveling down to an ant's eyebrow.

Under Norman DeVrees the pyramid fanned out a lot. Jackson Johnson was head stud groom; Pop was in charge of weanlings and yearlings; Perry Green took care of broodmares. Nancy Corbett was trainer in charge of starting the yearlings, and Lloyd Overholtzer was head trainer, in charge of racing stock.

Under each of them came the worker bees; that was myself, R. B. Bates, and about twenty other semiskilled types. I was an exercise rider under Nancy, R.B. was Jackson Johnson's assistant, and so on. There was a layer under us, mostly school kids and mentally handicapped guys, who cleaned stalls and mowed and weeded.

In the vast and horsey world of Tradition Farm, however, there was no place for a rising young television executive, which was what my mother was. That was one reason she left.

She had met Pop at a singles dance in Cincinnati while she was a secretary in a Cincinnati television studio. Pop was twenty years older than she was, and they had nothing in common, ever. I suppose he thought he was getting a Suzy Homemaker, and she thought she was getting a father figure, or

2

something. At any rate the marriage never did take, not really.

Pop never said very much about her after she left for California, for a higher-up job in the TV network. But I was ten then, old enough to know what he was feeling. Relief, mostly. Mom had spent eleven years making little digs at him because he wasn't as smart as she was and because he never wanted to do anything with his life but just take care of horses. I could see his point; but she never did, and I guess even a patient, easygoing man like Pop can take only so much belittling.

When she decided to take the California job, the two of them sat me down and asked me if I wanted to go with her or stay with Pop at the farm. I never want to go through a scene like that again. The reason it was so hard was that it was so simple, and it shouldn't have been. Pop and I were closer than mud on a boot, and I loved everything about Tradition and my life there. Mom had spent so little time at home while I was growing up that her leaving made a shamefully small hole in my life. I felt guilty about it for a couple of years, then got tired of the guilt and relaxed.

After that I led a life that lots of girls would have killed for: a beautiful horse farm, all the riding I wanted, and Pop loving me but giving me almost complete freedom.

At school I was in the accelerated Talented and Gifted program, which made the work fun instead of boring. But I was in a hurry to get out of school, partly because sitting still indoors was against my religion and partly because I didn't have boyfriends. Whatever my quote-unquote talents and gifts were, they didn't include attracting boys. That can be hard to live with, especially in a small high school where everybody knows who's going with whom . . . and who isn't. Ever.

So I avoided school activities, took extra courses to get through faster, and spent the rest of my time with the horses. At fourteen I was on the payroll, first as a stall mucker and hot walker, then as an exercise rider early mornings, before school. They started me with safe stuff, walking horses recovering from injuries, slow canters on broodmares to keep up their muscle tone, things like that.

By the time Pop died I was out of high school, thanks to the accelerated program, and was riding full-time on green yearlings and two-year-olds. It was the most dangerous kind of exercise riding because those adolescent babies had very little sense and even less experience under saddle, and any little thing could send them into orbit. Broken bones are a way of life for exercise riders.

On that night in May, three months after Pop's death, I was hobbling on a twisted ankle from an unscheduled dismount off a rearing filly. It wasn't as painful as a break, but it was no hangnail either. The ankle was tightly taped, and I was rattling with aspirin; but even so, it felt like an allover toothache whenever I moved. So I was annoyed when Casper went to the living room door and scratched and gave me that look.

"You were out an hour ago. Why didn't you take care of it then?" I snapped. He lowered his head and apologized with his tail but stood his ground. He was a white German shepherd, named for Casper, the Friendly Ghost in the cartoons. He belonged to the farm but chose to live with me in the apartment. Even though he was nine and probably didn't have the strong bladder of a two-year-old, it still seemed to me that his midnight urges were more recreational than vital.

I really did not want to move. I'd been dozing on the sofa with my sore foot on a pillow, a cat on my stomach, and an Agatha Christie movie just starting on the TV. I didn't have to ride at dawn, as I usually did—because of the foot—so I'd planned to treat myself to a late movie. I loved mysteries.

But Casper whined again and glared at me, so I grunted and shifted out from under the cat and lowered my foot to the floor. "Okay, buster, but you better have to go."

I opened the door and hobbled down the long, steep flight of stairs to the outside door at the bottom. Our apartment was the south half of the second floor of the old original farmhouse, limestone like all the buildings but softened by deep porches and forests of flowering bushes, lilac and azalea and honeysuckle.

I lowered myself to the porch step and watched, wryly, while Casper made a token salute to the gatepost, then sniffed away toward the stud barn, on the trail of a cat.

It was a gorgeous night, almost worth hopping down the stairs for. There was a full moon, but a blowing curtain of clouds hid it, so that it showed only through the sheer places in the sky. The air was warm and rich with the scent of flowers and freshly mowed grass.

An owl swooped past. My gaze followed it, then snagged on something wrong: a faint shaft of light rising from the roof of the breeding shed. It was a small, square building just beyond the stud barn to my left. The breeding shed was windowless, with

5

just a roof skylight for ventilation. It had been built that way for maximum shielding of temperamental thoroughbred stallions from distractions while they performed their multithousand-dollar rites.

Lights at night from the breeding shed were not unusual since Ambassador, our premier chief high mucky-muck stallion, was a little weird and refused to breed in the daytime. Too easily distracted by sounds and movements from outside the shed, Jackson said. As head stud groom, actually stud manager, he was in charge of breedings. The thing that made me curious was that it was late May, well past the usual February breeding season.

Since thoroughbreds all have official birthdays on January 1, a colt born in the summer is at a whopping disadvantage in two-year-old races, against competition six months more mature than he is. Gestation being eleven months, the best time to breed for January foals is February. May is a little too late.

I frowned and pondered. All of the Tradition Farm mares were bred and settled for this year. All the visiting mares had been served and sent back to their home stables except for a couple who—Oh. That was it. Two of the visiting mares had failed to settle from their first breedings and had stayed over until they could be rebred, vet-checked, and certified as pregnant. One of them must be in the breeding shed, I thought, for one last attempt with Ambassador.

One of Ambassador's sons, our own Attaché, won the Kentucky Derby last year and missed the Preakness by a whisker. Since then the world seemed to be full of mare owners waiting to book breedings to the sire of the Derby winner, and at prices that could feed starving nations. I supposed the owner of tonight's bride would rather have an April Ambassador foal than miss the year entirely.

I was getting tired of sitting, and Agatha was progressing upstairs without me, and Casper had disappeared into the stud barn through the cats' hole. Grumbling, I hoisted myself up and went after him. The main door to the stud barn was locked, as usual, but I figured I could get in through Ambassador's paddock, via his own private entrance into his stall, while he was otherwise occupied in the breeding shed, then grab Casper and go back to the movie.

I eased my ouchy self through the paddock rails, opened the top half of the stall door, reached in to work the lock on the bottom half. Something clamped around my hand.

I swallowed a shriek. It was warm, hard, damp, and was crunching the bones of my fingers.

A large, wet eye glittered at me: Ambassador. We recognized each other simultaneously, and he released his tooth-lock on my hand. I muttered an apology, closed the door top, and retreated to find Casper emerging through the cat porthole in the main door, bored and defeated and ready to go back to bed.

I let him in the downstairs door but turned, paused, massaging my bruised hand, then sat again on the porch step beside an overgrown azalea. Then it hit me. If Ambassador was in his stall crunching hands for recreation, then what was going on in the breeding shed? None of the other stallions had his penchant for night breedings, and that building wasn't used for anything else. At least it wasn't supposed to be. So why was that dim light still shining up from the skylight?

Curiosity overcame limp, and I eased around into the black-on-black shadow of the stallion barn toward the breeding shed door. I could hear low voices, but I couldn't tell whose. Hooves thumped on the tanbark within. I tried the door, but it was locked from the inside.

I didn't know whether that was standard procedure during a breeding or not. I'd never tried to spy on one before. Apprehension buzzed through me. If something was going on in there that shouldn't be . . .

I backtracked around the corner of the stud barn to watch. A breeding usually took less than twenty minutes, including the washing and disinfecting of the appropriate bits of horse, the tail wrapping, and the courtship. Any minute now.

Suddenly I realized I was standing in the path of horses being returned to the stud barn. If it was some other stallion in there, doing a breeding under Ambassador's name, and if I was caught watching . . . Chills raised my arm hairs, and I backed away again, this time to the house porch and its screen of shrubbery.

I had barely settled into watching position when the skylight darkened and the shed door opened. A double figure emerged, someone leading a horse. I couldn't see who. They plodded away in the opposite direction toward, well, toward anywhere, I realized: broodmare barn; colt stalls; any one of the fifty buildings on the place.

A second figure emerged, also leading a horse. I shrank, assuming this one was headed for the stud barn, but horse and leader disappeared in the other direction, around the corner of the hay barn and out of sight. I waited a few seconds, then followed, but by the time I got to the corner of the hay barn no one was in sight, man or beast.

Back in the apartment I turned off the television set and went to bed to think. Who needed television mysteries with funny stuff going on right here? I thought. I settled into my permanently unmade bed between the dog and the cat to ponder upon horses that weren't where they were supposed to be on a May midnight.

I was about to give it up and sink into sleep when a thought came rising out of the muddle and pulled me upright with it.

Tonight I had accidentally seen something that, very probably, no one was supposed to see. Three months ago, within a month of assuming his new duties in the stud barn, Pop had died, died a shameful, if accidental, death.

But what if he, too, had seen something he wasn't supposed to see, something involving three-hundred-thousand-dollar stud fees?

What if his accident . . . wasn't?

2

I got up almost as early as if I'd had to work and sat over my breakfast, staring into space and thinking. I had a good spot for it; the kitchen-living room had been the farmhouse's master bedroom in its previous existence, and it had a bay window that jutted out at the front of the house, with tall windows overlooking the stable area. The table sat in the window bay.

I was going to miss the apartment. It wasn't fancy, or even very big, just that kitchen-living room and two small rooms behind it, my bedroom and Pop's with a little bathroom jammed in between. Everything had been painted or papered in shades of brown, and the furniture was Salvation Army makeovers; but it had been home for Pop and me all these years, and it had been a good home. Full of goodtimes memories.

If I'd needed any new reasons for disliking R.B., the apartment would have done it. I was going to hate having to shrink my space down to a bed and chest in the women's dorm. I'd been in the dorm room, over the yearling barn, and it was a pleasant enough place for the half dozen stable girls and exercise riders who lived there, probably nicer than lots of college dorms; but I was used to space and privacy around me. It was going to be tough.

I knew I should spend the day sorting and packing for the move, but I couldn't get into it. Instead, I sat at the table, staring out the window and automatically fending off George, the cat, who was working his way across the table toward my cereal bowl.

That business last night. I couldn't get away from it. There had been, apparently, a breeding done in secret, and done by a stallion that didn't live in the stud barn. Who? Mentally I went over every building on the place, every horse in it. There were three young stallions among the two-year-olds, but they were being raced. Mr. Overholtzer would never allow them to be used for breeding while they were in race training. There was too much danger of their wanting to fight other stallions on the track once they started having a sex life. Of course, Overholtzer might not have known about it. That was a possibility. Okay, who else?

I was almost positive there were no other ungelded male horses on the place. Well, Toby, but he didn't count. Every other horse on the place was mare or filly or gelding, or living in the stud barn, and last night's horse had not been returned to the stud barn.

And beneath all of these questions, in the bottom of my mind, was a nagging uneasiness about Pop's death. It was separate from my grief, just an instinctive feeling that the facts didn't fit together.

I stared out through the leaves of the oak beyond the window. It was after eight, and the place was in full swing down there. I could see Nancy and two exercise riders coming in from the small track around the hayfield where the beginners got their first race training. Overholtzer and another knot of helpers and watchers were finishing the morning workouts at the main track, to the south, the one equipped with starting gate and bleachers. Stable help moved like worker ants, wheeling loads of manure and bedding, rolling up water hoses, hanging leg wraps out to dry in the sun.

Just below my window, Mrs. Jewett rode past on Toby, heading for the sandy lane that led back into the woods. She rode there most mornings. It was a great place to ride, pine forest, deer, wildflowers in the spring. The old logging road looped and meandered and made you want to see what was around the next bend, even if you knew the place by heart.

I frowned. Toby was a stallion. But it couldn't have been Toby. He was just a pleasure hack, not even a Thoroughbred. No reason to use him for illicit breedings.

Finally I got up and went downstairs, Casper grunting along behind me. This sneaky breeding business twanged on my instincts, and I couldn't shake the feeling that somehow Pop's death might be connected, illogical though that might seem on the surface.

Also, I wanted to avoid the sorting and packing job, as though I could avoid the move that way.

I stretched in the sunshine and wandered as casually as my sore ankle permitted into the stud barn. It was unlocked and open to the morning air, a small but elegant place, three huge stalls on each side of the central aisle, the tack room, the office where Pop had died. I seldom went in there, but this morning I ambled in, wondering what excuse I'd give if anyone saw me there.

The office was empty. On Jackson's desk lay his clipboard, with his daily work sheets on it, notations of medication, breedings, exercise schedules. Humming under my breath, I angled myself over the clipboard and lifted the top page. On yesterday's sheet, just below, was the notation "Ambassador to Mirror Image, 3pr."

I didn't know what the "3pr" meant, but Mirror Image was a visiting mare, one that hadn't settled on her earlier breedings. And whomever she was bred to last night, it wasn't the stallion her owners were paying three hundred thousand dollars for.

A toilet flushed, startling me. I was across the office by the pop cooler by the time the door opened to the little bathroom behind the office and Jackson Johnson came out, tucking in his shirttail.

To cover our mutual surprise, I said, "I was hoping you had some Orange Crush in this thing. I'm about out of groceries up there, getting ready to move." I lifted the lid of the cooler. It was an antique, the kind where rows of bottles hung by their necks in little tracks. It took a dime to release a bottle, but Jackson kept a supply of dimes there handy.

He was one of my favorite people on the place. A little guy, shorter than I was, and kinder than God. He looked like Popeye, with skinny arms and bowed legs and a bald head wreathed with wiry gray fringe. He and Pop had been two of a kind, old, leathery horsemen, constantly arguing with each other over unimportant things but maintaining a brotherhood beneath their hobby of bickering.

I fetched myself an Orange Crush, which I didn't really want since I'd just finished breakfast, but I didn't want Jackson to think I was sticking my nose where it didn't belong.

"How's the hoof this morning?" he asked.

I stuck out my taped leg. "No big deal. Couple of days and I can ride again." Quickly I decided to take a chance. "Hey, Jackson, I saw lights on in the breeding shed last night. You running a floating crap game in there these days?"

He chuckled, smiled, appeared unruffled by the question. "Nah, old Harold had a repeat breeding; that Image mare. She had a yeast infection before and didn't settle. This one should do it."

"Ah." I nodded. Harold was Jackson's pet name for Ambassador. "Well, back to work." I left the stud barn, ducking under the crosstie rope that held Ambassador in the center of the aisle. R.B. was bent over the stallion's near front hoof, gouging it with a hoof pick, while the horse eyed R.B.'s rear thoughtfully.

"Go ahead, take a bite," I muttered to the horse.

"Buzz off, cripple," R.B. said. He stood, letting the hoof drop. "And by the way, how soon are you going to get your junk out of that apartment? Mary Jean wants to get in there and measure for curtains tomorrow."

He was smallish and thin, with greasy hair straggling over his collar and eyes that bugged as though he were constantly surprised. I think it was a thyroid condition, but I couldn't like him well enough to feel sorry for him. If he'd been bigger, he would have been a bully. I was curious to see what kind of prize this Mary Jean was going to be.

"She can come and measure anytime she wants," I said. "I'll be out by tomorrow."

I was starting back toward the house, thinking I really should get the packing done, when Mrs. Jewett and Toby came out of the woods and trotted to a stop beside me.

14

I'd always liked her, maybe because she gave the impression that she liked me. She was probably in her sixties, but her hair was still bright metallic gold, piled high on her head. She wore frontier pants and a western shirt and expensive blue lizard boots, out of place on an Ohio thoroughbred farm but somehow right for her. Her face was lined and crepey, but as carefully made up as if she were expecting to be seen.

"How's the foot, Gusty?" she asked with genuine concern.

"Fine. Be riding again in a couple of days." I smiled up at her. Norman DeVrees came by with three tiny racing saddles over one arm. He looked at us, hesitated, stopped a few yards away.

"Well, you take as long as you need, dear," Mrs. Jewett said. "Don't you get back on those colts till you're a hundred percent, hear? You tell Nancy I said so."

I grinned. "I won't. I will. How was your ride?"

"Oh, fine as usual. Toby's having one of his lazy mornings today, though, aren't you, old darling?" She patted the horse's neck, and he shook his mane. Norman edged a step closer, openly listening to us now.

I looked more keenly at Toby. A lazy morning? No, impossible. It couldn't have been Toby last night. Toby was just . . .

He was a big, rawboned horse, black shading to brown on muzzle and flanks, fading to dark mahogany in summer. He had a quality head but a thick, unimpressive neck, an untrimmed shaggy mane and fetlocks, good legs under thickened body, much of which was hidden under the ornate silver-cornered western saddle and green-and-white rolled-edge pad. On his head he wore a bitless hackamore instead of a bridle, and across his chest like armor was a silver-mounted breastplate.

Without thinking I reached for his head, to stroke it. He jerked away, throwing his head as far as the tie-down allowed and rolling his eye at me.

"Sorry," I said. "I forgot he was head-shy. Where did you get Toby?" I made my voice sound casual, uncaring.

Mrs. Jewett smiled, including Norman in the smile. She steadied the horse with a pat of her diamond-crusted hand and said, "He was a gift actually. Norman gave him to me when my old horse Trigger died."

Conversationally I said, "What did Trigger die of anyway? I forgot."

"Colic. He was twenty-three, though. Slowing down. Three days later Norman drove in with Toby here, said he'd be perfect for me, and he was right." She smiled at him again.

I walked away, then turned back to look at them again: Mrs. Jewett bending down to look at something Norman was showing her on the underside of a saddle, Toby dropping his head for a snack. Something struck me about Toby then, something I'd never noticed before, probably because I'd never paid much attention to him. He reminded me of . . . whom? Big black-brown horse, no white markings, something familiar about his head—those small ears out of proportion to the rest of him. Who? I couldn't think.

Giving up the fragrant May outdoors with aching regret, I climbed the stairs, hesitated, came pounding back down again. Across the grass I hobbled toward the paddocks behind the stud barn. There in his private domain romped Ambassador: huge seal brown stallion, no white except for a tiny snip on his nose; small delicate ears with an almost Arab tilt to them.

He was bucking and romping around the paddock with all the vitality of a stallion who hasn't done a breeding in weeks.

Across the stable area Mrs. Jewett rode her hack toward the small private stable near the main house—her dark brown small-eared stallion hack who was having one of his lazy mornings. . . .

3

Ambassador's son Attaché was in the crossties, being polished by Jackson himself. This was the king, the Derby winner. No one but Jackson touched him. By now the morning was glaringly bright, so I paused within the barn while my eyes adjusted. Jackson, thinking he was alone, was singing under his breath.

Attaché was somewhat smaller and finer-boned than Ambassador, a medium chestnut, built more for running than catching the eye. It was just a year ago that he had won the most coveted, most glory-covered race in the country. Now he was retired to stud. He had served a full booking of forty mares this spring, results unknown for another two or three years. As Jackson and Pop used to say, never actually agreeing with each other but saying the same thing nonetheless, a winner on the track isn't necessarily a producer of winners.

"Jackson," I said tentatively, wondering how much to say.

He turned to me and grunted companionably but went on polishing Attaché, running the soft cloth around the horse's eyes, into nostrils and ears, playing with him as Attaché nipped at the rag.

"I just noticed something funny," I said. Casually

I drained the last of the Orange Crush so I could get rid of the bottle I was tired of carrying.

"What's that, Gus?"

"I was just talking to Mrs. Jewett and looking at Toby. You know who he reminds me of?"

Jackson selected a soft brush from the box on the side wall and began brushing Attaché's short, fine mane. "Who?"

"He reminds me of Harold. Did you ever notice that?" I tried to see Jackson's face beyond the horse's neck.

Jackson snorted. "That's because you're still a beginner at horses, even though you do think you know it all. All you're seeing is two big dark horses. Same coloring, nothing more than that."

"No, seriously, Jackson. Look at his head sometime. He's got the same kind of head and those same little ears."

"Ach." Jackson hacked and spit. "That Toby's a grade horse. He don't look nothing like Harold. What's bred in the bone comes out in the flesh. There ain't no breeding in that Toby horse."

I pondered, then risked a deeper question. "Jackson?"

"What?" He sounded cranky now.

"How did the breeding go last night?"

For an instant he said nothing. He moved to Ambassador's tail and began brushing, so I couldn't see his face. "Went all right. Damn fool question."

I started to say, "But Ambassador was in his stall. I saw him." I bit the words back, uncomfortably aware that Jackson had to be lying and that if something wrong was going on here, he must be in on it. I didn't want to believe that. And I shied away from exposing any more of what I knew to a man whom, suddenly, I wasn't able to trust.

I mumbled something about my imagination's getting out of hand and turned to leave.

R.B. was in the office door. Fleetingly I wondered if he'd overheard, but if he had, it apparently hadn't meant anything to him. He was, for him, cordial as he said, "Hey, Gusty, could you do something?"

"What?"

"Were you going into town for anything this morning?"

"Hadn't planned to."

"Well, listen, since you're too bunged up to work, I was wondering if you'd run a few errands in town for me. With the wedding coming up Saturday, and no time off to do this stuff," he said pointedly at Jackson, "it'd sure help me out. I've got to get my good suit to the cleaners, and I need black socks to go with it."

I sighed but couldn't think of a good enough reason not to go. There were a few things I wanted from town myself. And I wanted time alone, to think.

Fifteen minutes later I was on the road in the one thing that Pop had left me, our ancient Volkswagen Bug, formerly red, now mostly rust, and cruddy inside. The road was a winding, narrow blacktopped county highway, and the scenery was no less beautiful for being familiar: ripples of wooded hills, white-fenced pastures, and hayfields ripe for their first cutting. I loved this place. Even if I had to live in the women's dorm, it was still where I wanted to be in the world. I thought smugly how few seven-teen-year-olds are where they want to be . . . and know it.

Laurel wasn't much of a town, just two blocks of business district, but I made a miniature holiday out of the trip anyhow. I needed some distance between myself and the business about the stallions, as though answers might appear out of my subconscious if I didn't force them.

I did R.B.'s errands, poked through the paperbacks in the drugstore, hoping for a good mystery I hadn't already read, gave myself a squirt of the sample cologne at the cosmetics counter, and treated myself to lunch at the Eat-Rite Café across the street: tuna-salad sandwich on thin white and a watery Coke.

I was putting off going home, putting off the packing job and the thoughts about Jackson and the stallions. I drove home slowly, getting honked at by cars I hadn't realized were behind me.

The facts seemed pretty unavoidable. Some other horse was doing breedings under Ambassador's name, and much as I hated the thought, I couldn't imagine how that could be happening without Jackson's knowing about it.

I couldn't even begin to think why. Instead, I tried to concentrate on who. Who human, and who horse. Who human first. Mrs. Jewett? That kind lady in her silly clothes? She owned us all, Ambassador and any other horse on the place. If the ringer was Toby, then . . . Mrs. Jewett was the only person on the place who handled Toby. She even took care of him herself. I'd seen her, cleaning his stall, filling his water bucket. She laughed and made semijoking remarks about not wanting to lose touch with real life. For a woman with her diamonds, I'd always thought that was a little odd. You can keep in touch with real life without shoveling wheelbarrow loads of it every day. But I liked her better for doing it.

What would she have to gain from a stallion switch? Money, obviously, if there was some reason why Ambassador couldn't do the breedings himself, and she was making a third of a million per stud fee. . . . I shook my head. She just didn't seem the type.

Maybe Norman DeVrees then? He was the one who had given her Toby . . . if Toby was the ringer. He was Jackson's boss, had the power to fire Jackson if he didn't go along. But why would Norman do something like that? Money again? What would he get out of it? Stud fees went directly to Mrs. J. Unless he really was planning to marry her and was lining the nest. Mr. DeVrees wasn't one of my favorite people—he was too absolutely lacking in humor for me—but basically he was a straight guy, as far as I knew.

Who then? Who would be the type? R.B. was my least favorite person at Tradition, but for that very reason I veered away from suspecting him. It would be too easy to fall into that trap, suspecting someone just because I couldn't stand him. Besides, he was too dumb, too far down in the power structure. He'd have no way to make Jackson go along with it.

Jackson himself then? No. He was a decent, good man. If I knew anything about human nature, it was that. If Jackson Johnson were involved in any way with anything crooked, it would have to be against his will.

Who else then?

Who else?

I drove through the limestone gates and parked beside the house, my mind still working at puzzles.

I climbed the stairs and opened the living room door—and jumped.

Norman DeVrees was sitting there, in a chair beside the window, just sitting, looking at me with his hard eyes. He was a tall blond man, thickening at the waist, thinning at the hairline, always dressed as though he were playing the part of stable manager: tweed jackets, leather elbow patches; pipe unlit but used for pointing, like a stage prop. He was the only man I'd ever seen who actually wore silk stocks at the neck of his shirt.

"Hi," I said warily, not liking the way he was looking at me.

"Gusty, I'm sorry to have to say this, but you're fired. I want you out of here by tonight."

I dropped my purse and my jaw.

He held a roll of twenty-dollar bills toward me. It looked like a substantial roll. Confused, I thought he was paying me off, giving me my final pay in cash. Fired? I stared at him, still not comprehending.

With a voice like God he said, "I found this."

"What?" I shook my head, confused.

"This." He waved the money angrily. "I found this two hundred dollars in your dresser drawer, and I know where you got it. And this was wrapped around it."

He held out a small sheet of cheap lined notepaper on which was printed, in block letters, "Gusty, thanks."

"Where did that come from?" I asked. The question sounded false, even to me.

"You know where. You've been selling information."

"I've been what? Are you crazy?"

His face darkened. "Don't take that tone with me, girl. You can just be thankful I'm not calling the police about this. Oh, I knew it was going on. The Jockey Club has been on my back for weeks, in their quiet way, of course. Since Snowball in Hell."

Snowball in Hell. I frowned, trying to remember what I'd heard about him recently. Snowball was one of our two-year-olds, an unimpressive-looking gray colt, not one of mine. He'd run his first race a few weeks ago, surprising almost everyone by winning handily and paying fifty to one odds. The only people who knew his potential speed were the few of us here at Tradition who had seen his workouts. I'd heard some vague gossip about someone on the outside having apparently gotten word of Snowball's workout times and making a killing at the betting window.

I knew that information like Snowball's work speeds could always find a ready market among the touts and bookies, men who made their livings, and occasionally their fortunes, by knowing more about the horses in a given race than the betting public knew. I knew there were crooked stable workers who sometimes sold such information. As far as I knew, it hadn't happened before at Tradition, although there had been suspicious coincidences from time to time.

But nothing like this. No direct accusations, and certainly not aimed at me. I was so astounded I had to fight an attack of the giggles, the idea of my doing something like that was so ridiculous. For an instant I saw myself huddling in a raincoat with upturned collar, under a streetlight in misty rain, muttering from the corner of my mouth, "Snowball in Hell in the sixth," and receiving the payoff in a rolled-up newspaper. I couldn't help grinning.

"I'm glad you think it's funny," Mr. DeVrees said angrily. "Betraying the trust of the people who have employed you all these years, given you a home—"

"Oh, come on, Mr. DeVrees. I'm laughing because the whole thing is so silly. I don't know anything about that"—I waved toward the money, still pointed at me like a gun—"and I don't think you have any right coming in my apartment when I'm not home and making accusations like these. I most certainly didn't sell information to anybody about anything."

The giggles were gone now, and I was trembling mad and beginning to be scared.

Mr. DeVrees laid the money and the silly, damning note on the coffee table. We both stared at it as it slowly unfolded. "We can't tolerate this sort of thing, Gusty. I'm sorry, you've been a good rider for us, but we simply can't take chances with employees we can't trust. Now I know things have been a little rough for you since your father died, and maybe you needed the money—"

"Mr. DeVrees, I'm telling you, I didn't sell information. I don't know anything about that money, and if you found it in here, then somebody must have put it here. Probably whoever told you to look for it. Didn't you think about that possibility?"

He shook his head, almost sadly, I thought. "It's no good, Gusty. I heard it from more than one source and from people I trust completely. Now, I can't give you a recommendation for another job, under the circumstances, but I won't mention what you've done unless I'm asked directly. That way, if

25

you can get a job in another stable, you'll have a chance to stand or fall on your own, without this incident following you. Please pack your things and be out by this evening. Here's your paycheck."

He pulled an envelope from his jacket pocket and held it out to me. When I didn't respond, he dropped it, along with the roll of bills, on the coffee table. While I was trying to close my gaping mouth and say something that would stop this nightmare, he turned and tromped down the stairs, shaking the house.

I didn't say good-bye to anyone. How could I bear to? In one calamitous stroke I was losing job and home and family, dignity and honor.

When the car was jammed to the roof with all the bits of my life, I went back up the stairs for a last look. The money still lay on the table. I'd tucked my check away in my shoulder purse, but I didn't know what to do with the damned, damning bills. Finally I picked them up and fingered through them. Ten twenties. Two hundred dollars.

Did Norman DeVrees honestly think I'd risk everything I loved for two hundred dollars? I hated the sight of the bills. Still, I slowly jammed them into my jeans pocket. What else was there to do with them? Leave them on the coffee table for R.B.? Bitterly I told myself, I've paid enough for them. I might as well keep them. It occurred to me that I might very well need some living money. I still had no idea where I was going from here, what I was going to do with my life.

Slowly I turned and looked one last time around the room. I realized that I didn't even know what, if anything, in the apartment belonged to Pop, and therefore to me, and what came with the place. But there was nothing much I wanted to keep.

Except . . .

I walked over to the wall between the bedroom doors and squinted up at the picture there. I'd always loved it. It was a cheap, small print in a plastic frame; but, of course, that means nothing to a child, and I had loved it as long as I could remember.

Its name was written at the bottom in fancy "olde" English lettering: *The Stirrup Cup*. It showed a group of mounted riders milling before a stately mansion, with a pack of hounds among the horses' legs. The horses were elongated greyhound types with chopped-off tails. The riders wore hunt clothing, red coats, high boots, and long dresses on the ladies, who rode sidesaddle. Moving among the riders were servants offering up trays of drinks, apparently in a last-drink-before-leaving ceremony.

I remembered Pop looking at the picture with me when I was very small, so small I had to perch on his shoulders to see it. He had told me about fox hunting, about the riders taking a stirrup cup, hot buttered rum or something like that, just before setting out on the hunt. It became one of our little closenesses, not quite a family joke, just something understood between us. One more cup of coffee for him, a little more milk for me, before we went out to start our work. Our stirrup cups.

The picture before my eyes wavered and disappeared in my tears, and in its place came another scene. Horrible. Gray February dawn, Pop lying sprawled on the floor in the stud barn office, his face just inches away from the little bottled-gas space heater. Beside him on the floor, the empty liquor bottle.

The last stirrup cup.

4

The aloneness I'd felt when Pop died was nothing like what I felt now. My grief for him was deep and genuine, but there had been arms to cry in: Nancy's and Jackson's, even Mrs. Jewett's for a fleeting moment at the funeral. I knew, now, how much that support system meant to me. The center had dropped out, but I hadn't fallen into the hole it left. Friends had grabbed me and hung on until I got my feet under me again.

Now, suddenly, I was cut off from everyone. I drove with no sense of direction or destination. Tradition was the only place I was supposed to be; what was I doing driving up 52 toward Cincinnati at five o'clock on a Tuesday afternoon? Why wasn't I helping with evening stable chores, fixing supper, planning an evening canter through the pinewoods on one of the lead ponies? Such a beautiful evening . . . I should be on a horse.

My tears hardened inside me.

The highway was growing, widening as Cincinnati drew closer, outbound commuters thickening in the other lane. I felt uneasy. I'd never been a city person and didn't like driving in that kind of traffic.

To my right a motel appeared, a nice, long, low, white, fake-southern-mansion kind of place, balanced nicely between cheap and expensive. On an impulse

I swung in. Thirty dollars a night for a single. Almost viciously I peeled off two of the damning twenties from the roll in my pocket and bought myself a home for the night.

Supper came from the paper bag on the front seat of the car, my gleanings from the kitchen back home: Ritz crackers; peanut butter; an apple whose flesh was softening toward rot. I'd intended it for Fancy Free, my favorite of the yearling fillies I'd been schooling.

On the wall near the bathroom door was a tiny coffeepot on a heating element. I used it to make tea from the box of teabags I'd brought along. Supper wasn't a gourmet feast, but then it didn't have much appetite to contend with either.

The room was nice. Looking around from my nest in the middle of the bed, I thought I could be enjoying myself if I weren't there under such awful circumstances. If Pop had been there to share things with . . . But it was a nice room. Clean. Strip of paper across the toilet to prove it hadn't been used since its last disinfecting. Two big beds, cable television, a card on the desk to fill out if I had any complaints about the service.

I sucked up the last cracker crumbs of supper, took a long, sleepy soak in the bathtub with my taped ankle hanging out over the edge, then crawled into bed for some serious thinking. It was barely seven, still twilight outside, but I'd been putting off the thinking until I could do it undistracted by driving or anything else.

Thing number one: I was framed. I couldn't help smiling a little at the melodrama of the thought, but it was true anyhow. Somebody had planted that money and note in my apartment and told Norman

to go look for it, probably told him right where to
find it. Stupid Norman, didn't it occur to him to
suspect whoever it was who fed him that terribly
handy information?

Okay, who could have done it? Almost anybody
on the place, but most logically R.B., since he was
the one who sent me to town to run errands. Yes,
but they could have been legitimate errands. God
knows that suit of his was a mess, and if he was
planning to get married in it this Saturday . . . But
I'd been gone two and a half hours, plenty of time
for anybody to have seen me drive out, run up to
the unlocked apartment—nobody locked doors on the
farm during the day—stick the money in my dresser
drawer, and go tattle to Norman. Unless . . .
Norman planted it himself. Even easier.

Easiest thing in the world for him to say, "More
than one person told me you were guilty, kid, so
take a hike." And he had heard Mrs. J. answering
my pointed questions about Toby just before I went
to town. So it could have been Norman or R.B. or
anyone else on the place. Next question is, Why?

To get rid of me, obviously. Why?

Because I'd started asking questions about
Ambassador . . . and Toby?

Okay, thing number two: Some other horse on the
place was apparently doing breedings under Ambassador's name. Maybe Toby, maybe some other
horse, one of the two-year-olds. But my hunch was
Toby.

In that case, why? And who was Toby? And who
was behind it?

Thing number three: What did all this have to do
with Pop's death, if anything?

Okay, start with the apparent facts. Pop had died

from inhaling gas from the broken space heater. It had broken because he passed out and fell on top of it, knocking it over, knocking loose the canister of bottled propane at its side. The flame had gone out; the gas went on escaping from the canister; his unconscious face was just inches away from the copper connecting tube.

He had passed out because he was drunk. The county coroner, on his way to the proclamation of death by accident, had found Pop unquestionably drunk, with a blood alcohol level unsafe to light matches around.

But—and here I frowned and dug deeper into the bed—but Pop never drank. He never drank because he was a recovered alcoholic. When I was old enough to ask questions about why he never had a beer or a whiskey with the other men in the evening, he told me plainly that he had a sickness called alcoholism, which meant that any kind of liquor was like poison to him. It would make him unable to stop drinking until he was unconscious or dead, and so he never did.

He had started drinking when he was a child, he'd told me, because his dad thought it was cute. His dad was always drunk, and Pop, not knowing any better, loved the man and wanted to do everything Daddy did. He'd started out in life with a promising job as a trainer's assistant but couldn't control his drinking and was fired from job after job, each one worse than the one before.

The thing that finally scared him into getting help was a spell in jail, thirty days for drunk driving. He told me about it, told me that it wasn't the fact of being locked up, or the men he was in with, or the shame of the experience that scared him. It was the simple fact that there were no horses in prison. He suddenly realized he could be spending most of his life in jail, locked away from horses.

After that he straightened himself out with a strength and heroism I could only imagine. It took three years without a drink before he could convince old Mr. Jewett to take a chance on him, and then he'd started as a stable hand, proving over and over his reliability before he was allowed near the valuable horses. By the time he met and married Mom, he'd put twelve years between himself and that last drink, and by the time I was old enough for the subject, he had grown a deep, quiet pride in himself and his victory.

I knew what no one else at Tradition seemed to realize. He would never voluntarily have taken a drink, not a beer, not a glass of wine with a restaurant dinner, not a julep to celebrate a won race.

That was one reason Pop's death was so hard for me to accept, not just the loss of him, but the apparent facts of his death, the unacceptable, unbelievable fact of the alcohol in his blood.

It was as out of character for Pop to drink as for me to sell information from the stable.

Both were apparent facts, and as I lay there in the strange, hard, clean motel bed, these two facts joined hands and marched side by side through my head. Both were apparently true. Mine was a lie, a setup. Why not Pop's? Why not setups arranged by the same person, and for the same reason?

Because we knew, or were coming close to guessing, something dangerous to someone, something that could put that person in danger if it were disclosed.

But in what danger? Danger of discovery, of

losing a profitable racket of some kind? Danger of prison maybe? Maybe.

Thing number four: What was I going to do about it? I could slink away and leave everyone I cared about assuming I was a cheat and Pop was a drunk. I could go to Mom in California and try to fit myself into her life, probably unwelcomed. She might believe it was true about me, and about Pop. She hadn't even bothered to come back for his funeral.

I could start making the rounds of other stables, probably get a job eventually even without references, but I'd be starting as a beginner, at the bottom of the heap. There'd be none of the acceptance as family that I'd grown up with at Tradition.

I could hole up here, or somewhere cheaper, and try to find out who was behind this whole mess, try to get it all brought out so I could go back to Tradition, where I belonged, to get back into line for Nancy's job eventually, to work toward head trainer and a good, solid future doing what I loved.

Sighing, I pulled the extra pillow over my face and tried to disappear. Nothing was good. Nothing was going to be easy. Damn!

But considering the options, there seemed to be only one direction to go. Back to Tradition somehow.

Morning brought a better mood and a surge of energy. During the night the stallion business had been working itself out in my subconscious. While I breakfasted in the middle of the bed on more Ritz crackers and peanut butter, I decided.

First, concentrate on the other horse. Maybe Toby, maybe not, but the more I thought about Toby, the more likely it seemed that he was the ringer. Closing my eyes, I pictured how he would look if he were cared for the same as the racehorses. As a pleasure hack he was probably on a mostly hay diet. Change that to the concentrated protein feed that the thoroughbreds got and the fat would come off his neck and body. Then trim up his tail, pluck his mane out short and fine, clip up his legs, replace the bulky western saddle and cowboy hackamore and breastplate with a five-pound racing saddle . . .

Yes. It was possible. If that were done, he'd look very much like Ambassador. And under that kind of feeding, his placid manners would liven considerably, too.

I scowled thoughtfully. Would a thoroughbred stallion, especially one that was used at stud, really be a ridable pleasure horse in the daytime? Dr. Jekyll and all that stuff? A low-energy ration of hay with just a little grain would help. If the horse had a naturally kind disposition, it was barely possible.

Then, too, I knew what kind of rider Mrs. Jewett was; I'd watched her for years. I'd studied all the riders around me because I wanted to be the best. Mrs. Jewett was a sloppy rider. She rode to enjoy the scenery. Some horses took advantage of that kind of rider, while others seemed to respond to it by gearing down themselves. I'd known horses that would give a good rider all kinds of trouble but that would carry a teetering child as calmly as a Shetland pony would. If Toby were that kind of horse, then yes, it was possible that he might serve a mare at midnight and go for a quiet canter next morning.

He'd been tired yesterday morning. Mrs. J. had mentioned it. He was having one of his lazy mornings, she'd said. Had he, I wondered, been having lazy mornings regularly through the breeding season, mornings when his energy had been used for other purposes during the night?

And was he head-shy, I wondered, not because he'd had surgery to remove warts from inside his mouth, as Mrs. Jewett said, but because the identifying tattoo inside his lower lip had been removed in some painful way?

I packed my paper bag and checked out of the motel, knowing that if I were going to skulk around the countryside playing detective, I'd have to do it someplace cheaper than thirty dollars a night. I drove back to Laurel, the closest town to Tradition Farm, cashed my paycheck, and closed my tiny checking account, the three hundred and change left after the funeral bills.

The road toward Tradition tempted me, but there was no point in trying to go back there. What could I do, get another look at Toby? That wouldn't prove much. What I needed to do was to find out who he really was, work back at the puzzle from that direction.

Again I headed for Cincinnati, thinking vaguely that there would be records there, old newspapers, that sort of thing.

The timing. Concentrate on the timing. Toby had arrived at Tradition five years ago. If, for reasons I couldn't begin to sort out, he had been brought there for the purpose of doing Ambassador's breedings for him . . . Let's see. Ambassador had raced as a three-year-old when I'd been about eight or nine. I remembered going to Keeneland with Pop and Mom to watch him race, and she'd left when I was ten. Then, after one season of racing, he'd begun throwing splints in a hind leg, and Mrs. Jewett decided to retire him to stud. Ambassador had won his first three races, I remembered, had been hailed as one of the top three-year-olds of the season. Then the unsoundness had appeared, his Derby entry had been forfeited, and he'd come home to stud.

Pop was working with the colts then, so I hadn't paid much attention to the stallions, but I could remember the disappointment over Ambassador's first crop of foals. Some were good, but only if the mares were outstanding. The mediocre mares produced worse than themselves; the good mares produced no better than themselves. A prepotent stallion, I knew, had the power to improve on any mare, to produce offspring with his superior quality. And Ambassador started out, that first season, showing no promise as a sire.

Thinking back as I drove, I recalled the stable talk. Mrs. Jewett had paid five hundred thousand for Ambassador as a yearling at the Keeneland sale, the highest price for any colt sold there that year. But more than money was at stake: She had to justify the purchase in the eyes of her friends, other wealthy horse breeders who hadn't thought Ambassador worth the price.

He had started his racing career with enough speed to justify his price, but then he had broken down. He had begun his career as a stud by producing sixteen live foals, none of whom showed early speed in the pastures or in their yearling training.

But then, after a second year in which he was used only a few times because of the disappointing quality of the first crop of foals, Ambassador had been bred, a third season, to only three mares, all owned by Tradition. Of those three foals, one was Attaché, the Derby winner, one was an important stakes winner in Florida now, and the filly had won her maiden race in record-breaking time.

Were those three jewels really sons and daughter of Ambassador, as their pedigrees said, or was their sire Mrs. Jewett's nice brown pleasure hack? Toby had arrived just in time to have sired Attaché, if I was remembering my dates right.

If Toby had been run in as a replacement, it must mean that he had quality behind him. He couldn't have produced Attaché and the others without it. If that were the case, why sneak him in, in disguise? Why not simply replace Ambassador openly with a new stallion?

The traffic was making me nervous. I pulled off the highway, which was by now an interstate, at a rest stop and sat there rubbing the steering wheel and seeing nothing before my eyes but horses and muddles of facts that didn't make sense.

Who was Toby? Where had he come from, and via whom at Tradition? Was he stolen? That would account for the secrecy, but still, it didn't make sense. Mrs. Jewett was no more a thief than I was an information peddler and Pop was a drunk. At least, I didn't think so.

She had enough money to buy herself a new stallion when Ambassador flopped. Or did she? Mr. Jewett had died shortly before Ambassador's purchase, and he had been a heavy gambler, so possibly the place was not as prosperous as it seemed.

Suppose—suppose what Mrs. Jewett had was a stallion with the breeding and reputation to draw good mares, at fair stud fees, but that didn't have the genetic capability of living up to his advertisement. When his first colts became public, his value as a stud would drop to nothing, and the five-hundred-thousand-dollar gamble would prove an embarrassing and expensive misjudgment. It was Mrs. J.'s first purchase after her husband died, her first executive decision, so the humiliation would be deeper for her than it might otherwise be.

But suppose, somehow, she managed to get hold of another horse, equally good, that could do the Ambassador breedings in his name? She could justify the purchase of her expensive stallion, and the stud fees would come rolling in.

Back to square one. Who was Toby, and where had he come from? I screwed up my courage and aimed the rusty red Bug back into the flow of traffic heading over the overpass and down into downtown Cincinnati. I knew, roughly, where the downtown library was. That would be a start.

5

It was almost dark by the time I left the downtown Cincinnati library and began fighting my way out of the city. I knew where I wanted to go, south into Kentucky on Highway 27; but to get onto 27, I first had to get out of the city on Interstate 471, and it eluded me maddeningly. I could see it sailing overhead, but the one-way streets sent me in circles around it, never up onto it.

Boy, talk about your country girls, I told myself scathingly. I had so much in my head that I didn't want to lose, too much to think and drive at the same time. But it was nearly eight o'clock, I was starving, and I needed to fight free of the city.

Eventually I turned the magic corner and found myself on the entrance ramp, and within minutes I was across the river into Kentucky and sailing into open country. My goal was Cynthiana, which looked like about an hour's drive on the road map on the seat beside me. But I didn't need to get there tonight, preferred not to, in fact. The car was low on gas, and so was I, and I intended to go no farther than the first cheap-looking motel.

Finally I found one and checked in, although I didn't like the way the creep at the desk said, "Will you be alone?" He obviously didn't believe me when I glared at him and said yes. And the twenty-five he charged me wasn't as cheap as I'd hoped from the looks of the place.

The room was decorated in tin and plastic and concrete, the concrete part being the mattress. Everything was in shades of browns and grays and seasick green, and the rug had some very strange-looking stains. I treated myself to a hamburger at the café next door to fortify myself for the room and for another night of thinking.

From the inner depths of the back of the car I dug out a little steno notebook, the kind with the spirals across the top. It was left over from school, with too many empty pages to throw away. My cozy nest had no bathtub, only a flimsy plastic shower stall that wouldn't work with my taped ankle, so I did without cleanliness and just crawled into bed with the notebook and a can of Dr Pepper from the machine out front.

Into the notebook I transcribed the scribble of notes I'd taken in the library. I'd written it all on the back of a cash register slip from the grocery store, the only paper I could find in my shoulder purse.

"Wood Hill Farm, Cynthiana, Kent. American Express, Dec. 12, '81, fire, never recovered."

This was the sum total of my day's labor, the endless bending over the microfilm machine, scanning reproductions of page after page of the *Cincinnati Inquirer,* every paper for every day for most of that year. I'd centered my search on the early winter months, knowing that Attaché had been sired in February of that year and that Toby, if he was stolen from another stable, had probably been taken within a few months of that date. Leave time for the tattoo surgery, a little hiding out somewhere until something could be done to Trigger so that Mrs. J. would be in need of a new riding horse.

This is, I reminded myself, all assuming that my ridiculous and fantastic theory is correct and somebody at Tradition actually stole a horse, or arranged to have him stolen, just so he could be snuck onto Tradition in disguise, so that he could take over Ambassador's breeding jobs, under the table, so to speak.

I still was not at all sure the whole thing wasn't just crazy. Staring at the spiral notebook, running my pen back and forth over the spiral wire at the top of the page, I did my darnedest to make logic out of it. My brain was too tired to work very well, but I tried. Again. And again.

Okay, so Ambassador was an expensive dud. So what? What racing stable in the country hadn't had its share of disappointing colts? The owners didn't go out and steal a different horse to use under the dud's name. They swallowed their losses and hoped for a new star in the next year's colt crop or the next spring yearling sale.

No matter how suspicious the Toby situation might look to me, I couldn't picture nice rich old Mrs. Jewett doing something like that, not even to cover the embarrassment of having paid a record price for Ambassador. And if the place were in financial trouble after Mr. J.'s death, it seemed much more logical to me that Mrs. J. would simply have closed the stable. It had been her husband's toy, really, not hers.

And Norman DeVrees . . . I beat my pen against the spiral. It was hard to imagine his doing such a thing either, mainly because he seemed so lacking, not only in humor but in imagination. And what reason would he have? Even if he was hoping to marry Mrs. J., that didn't necessarily mean she was thinking about marrying him. And that would be the only way he could benefit financially from turning Ambassador into a money-making machine.

Unless—unless he'd done it as some sort of grandstand gesture to try to win over his fair lady. Nah. He'd never think of anything like that, and if he had, I couldn't imagine him doing anything violent to Pop. On the other hand, he'd certainly been in a hurry to get me off the place on a questionable bit of evidence. And of course, Norman, or anyone else at Tradition, might have had motives I didn't know anything about.

Another thing bothered me. How could anyone know, before he stole a horse, that it was going to sire a Derby winner and develop solid gold sperm? Impossible.

And what, specifically, had been done to Pop? The coroner had seemed certain that his death resulted from inhaling the bottled gas while he was unconscious from the blow on the head, which was due to his passing out while drinking. If all that was true, then the only thing that another person could logically have done to him was to get him started drinking, and how anyone could have accomplished that I couldn't imagine. Pop was the strongest person I'd ever known in certain areas, and drinking was one of those areas.

Wearily I turned off the brown tin bedside lamp and tried to find a comfortable position against the mattress. I faced the fact that very probably I was chasing shadows, that the whole thing was born in my imagination, and that nothing I could do or learn would get me back to Tradition or alter the facts of Pop's death.

But since I was out of a job anyway, and would soon be out of money, and since stable work was all I knew or wanted, I might as well try for a job at Wood Hill and see what I could find out about its long-lost stallion American Express. Probably he would turn out to have been a fifteen-hand gray instead of a seal brown seventeen-hander. Probably he had been recovered and was at this moment resting comfortably in his bed at home, which was more than I could say for myself.

I had disturbing dreams of wandering alone through some hostile place, trying to find Pop, and in the darkness I woke once, startled by my own calling voice. My face was wet with tears.

Gas station attendants in Cynthiana couldn't direct me to Wood Hill Farm, but when I asked the people at the feed mill, they said take 62 north again, toward Oddville, hang a right at the second road, and about six miles up that road, bear right at the Y.

I fiddled around in town for an hour or so, knowing that the best time to bother stable workers was in the comparatively lazy early afternoon, after the morning chores and workouts and training and before the evening feeding and cleaning. I spent fifty cents in a do-it-yourself car wash, hosing down the Bug for a good first impression. I unwrapped the support tape on my ankle and stood on it. Ouchy still, but not bad. I didn't want to apply for a job looking like a cripple. I dawdled over an early lunch at the McDonald's at the edge of town, working all the little puzzles on the paper place mats while I figured out what my approach should be.

I'd use my real name. There was no way to avoid that danger because I wouldn't be hired without my Social Security card. I'd just have to take a chance that no one at Wood Hill would make the connection. Ours wasn't a world where formal introductions were often made to the stable help, so if I did get hired on, and if people at Wood Hill did have a connection with someone at Tradition, I'd just have to hope they wouldn't hear my last name.

I decided not to trust anyone, not at first anyhow. If Toby was American Express, if he had been stolen from here, there was a good chance someone working at Wood Hill was involved. No sense sending up warning flares by letting anyone know who I was or what I was looking for.

That meant I couldn't admit to having actual exercise rider experience on a racehorse-breeding farm. It was too small a world, too many people knew one another, and we were, after all, only a hundred miles from Tradition.

Okay, then, where had I learned to ride? On my own horse. Say, I had a horse at home that was off the track, a Thoroughbred that had broken down for racing purposes but that I'd reschooled as a riding horse. I lived . . . where? Up north somewhere.

I dug the road maps out of the glove compartment and found a hometown. Hillsdale, Michigan. I . . . left home last week after high school graduation and drove down to Kentucky because I wanted to work with racehorses. That sounded believable. Half the girls who drifted in and out of the Tradition family had backgrounds like that. They grew up reading romantic books about the wonderful world of horse racing, jumped into it for a while, got bored with mucking out stalls, and drifted on to something else. Or stayed and worked their way up to riding, sometimes even to jockeying. So I should have no trouble passing for one of them.

Wood Hill was aptly named. The private road led up a slight incline, through tree-dotted pastures, toward a more densely wooded crest where the main buildings were. The house was a glorified log cabin, accent on the *glorified*. It rambled along the hillside with wings at varying levels and decks and terraces everywhere. I drove past it. Owners' houses had little to do with my end of the business.

The stable complex was of varnished-log construction, too. The buildings were all low and rambling like the house and set in no discernible pattern. I parked near some other cars nosed into what looked like Old West hitching rails and went in search of the office.

The first person I met was a woman who reminded me instantly of Nancy: tall and stringy and tan-haired, with skin and features and haircut all aggressively masculine. She could have been thirty or sixty or anywhere in between. Although she was carrying a bucket of smelly, pus-encrusted leg wraps, I figured her for something higher than stable hand.

She stopped when she saw me, then approached as though she already knew more than she wanted to know about me and what I was there for.

"Hi," I started cheerfully. "Who do I talk to about getting a job here?"

"You talk to me, if you can catch me." She walked away toward a nearby building, and I fell in

46

beside her. The door she opened led into a sort of utility room, where an oversize washer and dryer both were doing their dances. After dumping the leg wraps into a hamper, she turned around, collided with me, sighed as though her load were too much to bear.

"Okay, what's your name, and what makes you think you can do us any good?"

She was already halfway across the graveled area toward another building, a stable. Quickly I said, "Gusty McCaw, I just graduated from high school, I've been riding all my life. My last horse was a thoroughbred off the track, and I reschooled him for pleasure riding and a little jumping. I love thoroughbreds, and I want to be a trainer eventually; but I know I have to start at the bottom, and that's okay, I'll do anything."

We were inside the stable, where a horse stood crosstied in the aisle, a new bandage on his foreleg. "Ugly gash he's got," the woman said, either to me or the boy on the other side of the horse. "Sliced himself on a loose rear shoe. Got a terrible overreach. If you were taking care of him, what would you do about it?"

I guessed she must be talking to me since the boy beyond the horse wasn't answering. I said, "I'd have noticed the shoe was loose and told somebody in charge so the farrier could pull the shoe and reset it before he cut himself on it. And I'd keep bell boots on his front feet when he was exercising."

She bent to test the firmness of the bandage, then motioned for the boy to put the horse away. She slapped the brown neck as she turned to me, finally looked at me.

"You do drugs?"

I flushed and shook my head.

"You pregnant or anything?"

"Of course not." She was making me mad. I wasn't used to people who didn't know and respect me.

"Just asking. Don't get your bowels in an uproar. Kids drift in here with all kinds of mess-ups, and they always seem to ricochet off onto me. Okay. Look, we can use another hand with the mares. You won't be riding. You won't be going to race meets. There's not going to be anything fun or glamorous about it."

She was warning me. I grinned.

"Minimum wage," she went on. "Six-day week, alternate Saturdays and Sundays off, working hours are dawn till suppertime, but we don't do much in the afternoons. My name is Chris, you take your orders from me, but Sherry will show you what to do. Go over to the mare barn, that's that long one with the green roof, tell Sherry you're her new assistant, and she'll show you where you'll sleep. Come over to the office after supper, and I'll get your Social Security number. You got one?"

"Yes. Thanks. Thanks!" I grinned with all the happiness of the fictitious Gusty McCaw from Michigan, about to start her first stable job. The happiness was genuine, even if nothing else was. As I jogged toward the mare barn, I told myself that even if nothing ever came of the Toby-Ambassador business, at least I'd landed in a decent place, with a job and a home. Things could be worse.

6

Actually things were worse. Oh, not the obvious things. The people I worked with were, on the whole, pleasant to me, the work had its share of bright moments, and the accommodations were probably better than average, better than I'd have had in the women's dorm at Tradition.

I lived with Sherry and two other girls, in a room in a building known as the bunkhouse, in keeping with the log cabin motif, I figured. The building was long and low and log, three large rooms: in one end our room, in the other a similar one—I guessed—for the single men, and in the middle a buffer-zone room, with kitchen and comfortable chairs, television, and pool table. It wasn't a home in the sense that our old apartment had been, but it was nice enough. If I had been what I pretended to be, a beginner in the business, I'd have been in hog heaven at Wood Hill.

But the strain of pretending to be less than I was was surprisingly hard on me. I'd grown up expecting to be better than the stable help; I'd started work at the rider level without ever giving much thought to the dozens of stable girls who came and went at Tradition, all hoping to be promoted to riding, a privilege I'd assumed as my right.

And I'd been good at it. That knowledge was the

main hook on which my self-respect hung, and now, suddenly, that was gone, too, along with Pop and the only home I'd ever known. The only way I knew to get through the moments of black misery that pounced on me when my guard was down was to work myself to exhaustion, day after day.

At first I didn't realize that by doing that, I was courting trouble from another direction: Sherry.

She was a round-faced young woman with rather flat, unattractive features and long, limp pale hair. I guessed her to be in her early twenties. She'd been at Wood Hill for several years, having run away from pressuring parents during high school. She had a love of cheap cologne, which went oddly, I thought, with her chosen profession, and she spent her evenings maneuvering for the attention of the guys in our communal living room.

At first Sherry accepted me with what seemed a mixture of relief that I wasn't gorgeous; eagerness to have me as a helper, admirer, and potential friend; and wariness that I might turn out to be a competitor.

Within a few days the wariness won out, and she began a campaign probably aimed at putting me in my place. The harder I worked, the more she found for me to do, and the more I did, the more fault she found with it. Once or twice I snorted in disgust at her attitude, and she caught me at it and grew red-faced with fury.

Luckily for me, Sherry had little actual power. Chris was our boss, and Sherry and I were more or less equal co-workers, her ascendance being only a matter of seniority. I tried to ignore her when I could and to get on with my work.

Sherry and I were in charge of the broodmares

and their few-month-old babies. In charge, that is, as a motel maid is in charge of her rooms.

There were sixteen mares, all belonging to Wood Hill. Since the stable owned no stallion, there were no outside mares, belonging to other stables, coming in for breeding, as there had been at Tradition. All the Wood Hill mares had been shipped away for breeding early in the winter. They had done their foaling at the stables of their mates, in order to take advantage of the thirty-day heat, the most advantageous season for breeding a mare, thirty days after foaling. Since the foals would be too young to travel at that age, mares were sent to their studs well before foaling date and came back to their home farms only after this year's babies were big enough to travel and next year's pregnancy was far enough along to be vet-certified.

At this time of year the stable work was light because mares and foals stayed out in pastures during the daytime and came up at night into a paddock, where a loafing shed offered protection in case of rain. The mare stable was used for only a few mares at a time, to confine them if something was wrong with them or their foals or to keep them safe during the weaning process.

Sherry and I spent our time in several ways. Twice a day we cleaned the occupied stalls, carried feed to the inmates, and saw to the automatic watering system. We raked the alleyways and kept the equipment—buckets, grooming tools, neck straps that the mares wore for identification—clean and in place.

We also walked out among the mares and foals several times a day, checking to be sure no one was injured or in trouble. Sometimes a foal tried to nurse from the wrong mama and got kicked; sometimes the foals, in their mad chases around the pasture, failed to stop or turn in time and crashed into fences or trees.

One morning I noticed a mare driving her baby away from her teat with vicious kicks and flattened ears. With some difficulty I caught her, tied her up, and looked underneath. Her udder was swollen and discolored in what appeared to me to be an unhealthy way, so I showed it to Chris. She called the vet immediately and praised me in front of Sherry.

After that things got even cooler between Sherry and me. I shouldn't have minded, but I did. Sherry wasn't anyone I'd have chosen for a friend, but it galled me to be disliked by her.

And it galled me not to be riding. On those misty early mornings I stood in the stable doorway, wheelbarrow full of manure balanced between my arms, my eyes following the clots of exercise riders and trainers jogging off down the hill toward the training track. That was where I belonged. Not here.

Grimly I told myself I was here for a purpose, and the stable work was just my cover. I had visions of leaving this place for something far better, preferably my old job at Tradition, or at least in some way letting Sherry and the others know who and what I really was. Especially Chris. My liking and respect for her grew daily, and I knew we would have been friends if only she could see me as I really was.

I waited a few days until I was settled into the routine and, I felt, accepted by the others. Then I began asking what I hoped would appear natural questions. First, Sherry.

"How come they don't have a stud force here?

This is a big enough place to have its own stallions, isn't it?''

She shrugged. "Don't ask me. I'm not on the executive committee around here." She had begun a sort of belligerent putting down of herself to me, as though daring me to agree with her. I just matched her shrug and tried another source.

Of the men and boys who lived in the other end, Randy seemed the most approachable. Not the most likable, just the easiest to start a conversation with. Randy was probably twenty-five or so and good-looking in an overadvertised kind of way. He had long hair that he combed a lot and impressive arm and chest muscles that he seemed to flex more than was strictly necessary. His hair was blond and wavy, but there was nothing feminine about the rest of him. He reminded me of the football players in school.

When I first showed up, he hit on me but in such an automatic way that there was nothing personal in it at all. He seemed to be using Standard Approach No. 3, for girls who were between foxes and dogs, good enough to want as admirers, not good enough to want as actual girlfriends.

I had laughed him off, and he, shrugging at my lack of taste, hadn't bothered to pursue me. There were others among the guys that I probably would have liked better, but they were harder to get to know. One or two seemed to be painfully shy, the type that loves animals because they're easier than people. A couple of others were going with someone, one was engaged, and their attitudes seemed to be saying, "Sorry, kid, you can't have me, I'm taken." Then there were three who appeared to be mentally slow and who clung to each other's company exclusively.

On Sunday evening I saw my chance and jumped in. We'd all had an easy day, and the heat lasted well into the evening, slowing us down even more. By suppertime the lounge was almost empty. Several of the guys had gone into town for the day, as had Sherry. I was on duty, but I'd finished by six and made myself a BLT for supper.

Randy and I were alone in the lounge, I with my sandwich at the kitchen table, he slouched in front of the TV. "Sixty Minutes" was on, and he appeared to be watching; but I had the feeling he was merely facing the screen, too tired or too lazy to move.

Then another program came on, and he got up, stretched, slouched over to the table, and dropped down across from me.

"How come you didn't go to town with the rest of them?" I asked, picking up a shard of bacon from the plate and eating it.

"Ah, all they do is waste their time and money, going to town."

That surprised me a little. I hadn't figured him for the conservative type. I teased: "What better do you have to do with your time and money?"

"Oh, you'd be surprised," he said archly.

"Try me."

"You really want to know?" He leaned back in the chair and looked down at me.

"Sure." I didn't care, but I did need to find out as much as I could about everybody here, including Randy.

"I've got plans. I'm not going to be a crummy

stable hand all my life. I'm saving up for a physical fitness center.''

"A what?'' That one came out of left field.

"You know, exercise equipment, saunas, fancy place with membership cards and all that. It's going to be all mine, and I'm not going to have to take orders from anybody, ever again.''

"Gee, that sounds great,'' I said weakly. "When is all this going to happen?''

"Just as soon as I get a few thousand more socked away.'' He went on telling me much more than I wanted to know about Nautilus equipment and handball courts, while I tried to find a way to get him back onto the subject.

"How long have you worked here?'' I got in finally.

"Six, seven years.''

"Tell me one thing,'' I said, deciding to plunge right in, "how come they don't keep any stallions here? I always thought a breeding stable—''

He shrugged. "I guess it's just more economical not to. Top winners don't come along very often, and the big-name studs are available anyway.''

"Like Ambassador?''

I couldn't tell whether something flickered across his face or not. Just my imagination, I decided. "Sure, Ambassador, Ruling Class, any of those.''

"Didn't this place ever have studs?''

"They had a good one a few years back. American Express. Ever hear of him?''

"I think so. Whatever happened to him?'' Carefully I kept my face blank, my voice even.

"Died. They had a stable fire—''

"He died in the fire?'' That wasn't what the newspaper had said.

55

"No, not in the fire. He got out, him and three others, when the stable started burning. They found the rest of them out in the woods afterward. Found American Express a while later, up in the hills someplace, dead with a broken leg."

My first reaction was crushing disappointment. If American Express had died in the hills with a broken leg, then he obviously wasn't Toby, who was alive and well at Tradition. My whole theory was the nonsense I'd originally thought it was, and . . . what was I doing in this place?

Through the long twilight and well into dark night I sat outside on a flat-topped log that edged the parking area, staring at nothing and trying to sort through my thoughts.

What other possibilities were there? That the unknown horse that Toby used to be was one I didn't know about. But if he had come from anywhere in the Ohio-Kentucky area, his disappearance would surely have been noted in the paper. This was too horsey an area, and stallions of that caliber represented too much money to go unnoticed by the press. He could have come from some other area, of course.

Or somehow my timing might be screwed up. He might have been stolen, or whatever, much earlier than I'd figured.

Or else there was something I didn't know, and needed to, to make sense out of it all.

I was still sitting there when the carload of guys came back from town. They lifted hands at me in greeting but filed into the building mostly uninterested in me, except for the last one in line, one of the extremely shy younger guys, Bobby. He was big and dark-haired and soft-looking, slow to speak but warm and genuine when he smiled. He came back and sat down beside me.

We talked a little bit: Where did I come from and where did he come from and had he worked here a long time? Yes, several years, he said. Did he have a nice time in town tonight? Yes, they'd gone to a movie and out for beers afterward.

Figuring that I had to stick my neck out a little if I was ever going to find out anything, and figuring Bobby for a gentle soul unlikely to be mixed up in anything rough, I plunged right in. "Bobby, were you here when American Express was here?"

His face saddened. "Oh, you mean Mutt."

Mutt. It had often struck me in the past that the greater the horse, the humbler his nickname. It was as though those who worked closest to him were superstitiously leery of giving him greatness in his name, for fear of drawing bad luck to him. Ambassador was Harold to those who cared for him. Attaché was Jiggs. American Express had been known to Bobby only as Mutt.

"Who took care of Mutt?" I asked.

Bobby smiled, remembering. "I did. See, I'm good with stallions because I'm strong, and I move kind of slow, so I don't spook them. Mutt was mine, and we had two other stallions then, too, but they weren't as good as Mutt was, and they were sold after the fire."

"What did Mutt look like?" I asked casually.

"Oh, brown. He was a brown horse. Big one."

My interest quickened. "Dark brown, you mean, or light?"

"Oh, real dark. Black in winter, just about. He was a nice horse. Never tried to hurt me. Some of those stallions, they like to take a chunk out of you if they get cranky, but my old Mutt never would.'' Bobby's voice thickened.

I left him then and went in to bed, to sort once again through my tangled thoughts.

On one hand, Randy said American Express had died. On the other hand . . .

She had warts, I interrupted myself, needing the relief of silliness. Pop used to say that. On the other hand . . . she had warts. Made no sense.

God, I missed him.

7

On the other hand, I woke thinking, on the other hand, Bobby's description of American Express sure didn't rule him out as the possible Toby. I wondered if there were photographs of him.

I spent most of the morning in a large, deeply bedded stall with a four-month-old filly who was taking the weaning process harder than most. She alternately stood, head down in the center of the stall, looking miserable, or made mad dashes back and forth, rearing, trying to climb the sides of the stall. Miraculously she made it through the morning hours uninjured, and by noon she was spending most of her time standing beside me, pressing her head against my chest and leaning into me.

About one Sherry, who had done all the morning stall chores, came to relieve me of baby-sitting duties, and I went home for a sandwich. Still chewing the last of it, I detoured past the office, which was in its own log cabin, and found Chris there doing desk work. I opened the screen and stuck my head in.

"That Baysfield filly sure does want her mama," I said.

Chris looked up, her long, horsey face creasing in a smile. "Is she okay?"

"She was quieting down when I left for lunch a

little while ago. Sherry's with her, but I think the worst is over. She was eating a little."

"Good. Gusty? How are you liking it here so far?"

I came in and let my eyes sweep the walls. Predictably they were covered with win photos from racetracks.

"Fine," I said.

"No problems with the work or the people?"

I shook my head.

Chris shot me an aw-come-on look and said, "You're really content doing this kind of work?"

"For now," I said cautiously. "Why?"

Chris shrugged and looked down at her schedule sheets. "No reason. I just don't figure you for a permanent stable hand. You've got too many smarts for that."

I grinned. She was easily my favorite person at Wood Hill, and her opinion of me was important. I wanted her for a friend, and one of the worst aspects of my present situation was the fact that I didn't dare let a friendship start or even let her know that I wasn't really a stable hand type of person. Then I grew uneasy. I knew I wasn't a stable hand, but how had she known so soon? I'd better be more careful not to let more expertise show through than I was supposed to have.

Chris looked as though the conversation were over, so I said, strolling along the wall of photographs, "You used to have a horse—what was his name?—he won some big race in Florida six or seven years ago. . . ."

She was looking at me blankly, so I went on, winging it. "I saw a picture of him in a racing magazine, and I remembered the name Wood Hill

Farm. I guess it kind of stuck in my mind, kind of a kid daydream, you know? I used to look at that picture and try to picture what a racehorse-breeding farm would be like. That's why I came here first, looking for a job. But I can't quite remember the horse's name. MasterCard, was that it? I was just kind of, you know, thinking about him, about that picture I used to look at.''

Chris rose and came around the desk. I tried to see if there was anything guarded about her expression, but she turned away from me, toward the opposite wall.

"American Express. This was probably the picture you saw. It was in all the magazines. He won the Flamingo Stakes at Hialeah in 'seventy-six. He was the biggest winner we ever had.''

I moved close to the photo and squinted at it. Sunlight glared on the glass, so that I had to tilt the frame. It was an eight-by-ten black-and-white print, showing a large dark horse standing in a winners' enclosure with jockey aboard and trainer and owners beside him, everyone grinning. A huge trophy hid much of the horse's neck.

I peered closer, conscious that Chris was watching me. The horse did have a smallish pair of ears, and he had no white markings that I could see. But when I tried to imagine him older and fatter and shaggier, with thickened neck and western tack, I just couldn't tell. Maybe, maybe not. I just plain couldn't tell.

"What happened to him?" I asked as casually as I could.

"Died," Chris said shortly. "We had a stable fire, and he got out and broke a leg up in the hills. We found him dead up there.''

"You're sure it was him?" I said, sticking my neck out another dangerous foot or two.

She looked at me oddly. "Of course it was him. Who else would it have been? Besides, he had his nameplate on his halter."

"Ah." I nodded. "Gee, that was too bad. I bet you hated to lose him. Had he sired any colts yet when he died?"

"Just two. We were still racing him so he wasn't officially at stud yet, but the two he did produce were gorgeous things. Both stakes winners, Apple Pi and Cortage, over there." She showed me more photographs.

"Well, back to work," I said finally, and escaped to the privacy of my work, where I could think.

Sherry was watching for me from the stable doorway as I came out of the office. "What were you doing in there, making points with the boss?" The unpleasantness in her voice was unsuccessfully covered with a layer of forced lightness.

"No, Sherry." I sighed. "I was just letting her know about the filly, and we got to talking."

"About me?"

I stared. "God, no. Why would we be talking about you?" Then I flushed, realizing how that might have sounded to someone as ready to be insulted as she was.

Sherry's round face darkened. "You just remember one thing," she said, "Chris and I are good friends. You got that?"

She seemed to be waiting for an answer, so shrugging to myself, I said, "Sure. You and Chris are good friends. So what?"

"So you stay away from her. That's all. Your job

is here in this barn, not in the boss's office. That filly needs more sweet feed, and you better stay with her for the rest of the afternoon. If she hurts herself in that stall, it's going to be your fault. You just keep your nose out of things that aren't your business."

Smiling on the outside, swearing on the inside, I went into the stable past Sherry's glower. This was more than ordinary worker rivalry, I thought. What was bugging her anyway?

Then it came to me. Sherry had some sort of crush on Chris and saw me as a potential threat. Good Lord.

Or. Or Sherry was in on the American Express thing and didn't want me asking questions. I wasn't sure which way I'd rather think of her, childishly jealous or potentially dangerous. Having to be suspicious of everyone around me was becoming a pain.

I picked up the scoop from the lid of the feed bin in the aisle, opened the bin, and reached far down inside it to corner the last of the sweet feed, a crumbly mixture of grains and roughage and molasses. Have to refill the bin, I thought.

The scoop came up, bringing feed and a dead rat. I smothered my yelp and steadied myself. Dead rats were nothing new in my life, but they were still yucky, especially unannounced.

This one was extremely dead, a flattened, papery wisp of brown and bone, the flesh all long ago disintegrated. I buried it in the manure pile deep enough to foil cats and dogs and threw out the scoop of feed with it.

After a quick look at the filly, who was stretched out on the stall floor asleep, I scrounged around in the kitchen and tack room, got a soup-can lid and hammer and nails, crawled into the feed bin and covered over the rat's entrance hole with the can lid. Then I hauled out a new fifty-pound bag of feed, wrestled it into the bin, and took a scoop to the filly's box.

It was a steamy hot afternoon, and was I running with sweat, so the prospect of baby-sitting in this comparatively cool stall for the afternoon wasn't all bad. I'd rather have been back in the lounge, where Sherry was watching soap operas and drinking nice cold pop, but on the other hand . . .

On the other hand, she had warts.

On the other hand, I didn't want to cross Sherry any more than I had to.

The filly scrambled to her feet and buried her small nose in the sweet feed, playing with it as much as eating it. I sat down in the wood shavings, leaned my back against the stall wall, and tried to think. After a few minutes the filly lowered herself, too, and went back to her nap, her neck across my ankle.

I was thinking about the dead horse up in the hills. He was wearing American Express's halter, okay, but that didn't necessarily make him American Express. Suppose it were another dead brown horse wearing the labeled halter.

Going over Chris's words, I frowned a little. Odd that she said, "Of course, it was American Express. Who else would it be? He was wearing the halter." Why hadn't she said, "It was American Express; he had the identification tattoo on his lip"?

Okay, suppose it were a different horse up there, posing as American Express. Whoever was doing all this could, I supposed, have had the ID number tattooed in the fake American Express. I had no idea how the tattoos were done, or by whom, but it seemed possible to me. But still, there would have been so many other ways a horse would be recognized, especially by the people who took daily care of him.

Bobby. Was I going to have to suspect that sweet, gentle guy, along with everyone else? Fiercely I hoped not. I liked Bobby. He might not be one of the most ambitious guys around, but he was a friend of sorts. And damn it, I was getting tired of having to suspect everyone. Chris, Bobby, people I genuinely liked.

The trouble was, Bobby was Mutt's groom, the one person who would never be fooled by a ringer. So either he was in on it, or . . .

Then I remembered the rat. The rat had been dead awhile. I had no way of knowing how long, but awhile. Weeks or months anyway. And there was very little rat left, just wisps of skin and a framework of skeleton.

A horse was much bigger, of course. It would take longer. But how long? I wondered. How long before a dead animal, even a large dead animal in the wild, with scavenging animals and insects aplenty to do Ma Nature's cleanup work, how long before that animal would be unrecognizable, except in a general way as a large brown horse? Even the parts that proclaimed him a stallion rather than the more common gelding would be among the first parts to go. And lips, tattooed or not.

All it would take would be a horse similar in size and coloring, a remote enough place that he wouldn't be discovered until Ma Nature had had a good go at him, and the name-tag halter saying "American Express." Probably the remains wouldn't even be examined very closely. If there seemed nothing suspicious about the death, there would be little reason to look beyond the halter, the skeleton.

If someone, probably someone working here, were connected with someone at Tradition Farm, and together they had cooked up the substitution scheme, and if the Wood Hill person had started a stable fire some night in the stud barn, easy enough to do . . . If he . . . or she. Or she? If he or she had led American Express away first—not hard to do for someone who worked here—and hidden him out someplace safe, then come back and started the fire, called for help, let the other horses loose, helped put out the fire, helped hunt for the lost horses . . .

Maybe had driven away later and taken American Express someplace secure, taken the substitute horse wearing the name-tag halter up into the hills. . . . I didn't want to think about that part of it, the poor substitute horse whose leg was probably broken deliberately for the sake of the plan.

And then, after tattoo-removal surgery, there had probably been a layover period in the security place, while—my mind was racing now—while Norman DeVrees or whoever it was arranged to colic the elderly Trigger. Again, not hard to do if you know horses. Then, presto, Toby appears as Mrs. Jewett's new riding horse.

Could it have worked that way?

American Express would have been an excellent choice for the switch. He was similar to Ambassador, a cousin if I had my pedigrees right. One of the pictures Chris had shown me in the office was a full-page ad in *Turf* magazine, showing American Express and his pedigree. I'd glanced over it, afraid to show too much interest. I liked Chris but wasn't ruling out anybody. My glance had told me that the grandsire of American Express, like Ambassador, had been Secretariat but that the parents of both stallions had been different individuals. So they were cousins, with enough family resemblance to make the offspring of one passable as the offspring of the other.

And American Express had already proved himself a sire of winners. Just what Tradition Farm needed, instead of the expensive dud it was stuck with.

If only I could find a link between the personnel here and back home. I pondered how to go about that, and all I could come up with was to throw off my cover and let it be known that I was from Tradition. That might cause a response, something I could go on.

I sat on that stall floor, absentmindedly stroking the filly's neck and wondering what I might be letting myself in for if I made that move.

Whoever had done this stallion switch, if indeed it had been done, was smart. And he—she—they had an awful lot at risk if the truth came out. How far would they go, I wondered, to keep me quiet if they thought I was a danger to them?

I thought of Pop again, and chills played up and down my back.

What should I do? My cowardly side argued that what I should do is take this to some authority. Police? Jockey Club? Somebody better able to handle it than I was.

But I smiled wryly, imagining the belly laughs my story would provide if I tried to sell it to the police or Jockey Club officials, as it stood now.

No, I was going to have to find out more on my own first, something definite to take to them.

Once again I tried to marshal my plans into some sort of workable order. I would talk to Bobby again, and maybe Chris, about the time span between the fire and the discovery of the body.

I would try to learn something from Bobby about American Express, some way of identifying him that I might be able to test on Toby.

I would try to find out, by exposing myself, who it was at Wood Hill that was connected in any way to Tradition Farm, and who the connection was at Tradition.

And what will you do in your spare time? I teased myself.

The clangings of evening feed time roused me from the floor and answered my question. In my spare time I'd better do my job.

I dusted off my jeans and went to the paddock where my filly's mom and three other newly separated mares were milling uncomfortably, milk oozing down their hind legs. I slung a bale of hay into the cart and wheeled it to the mares and spread it so they didn't have to fight one another for it.

Ah, the glamorous life of a girl detective.

I was still laughing, just a little, at my pretensions. Even the idea that I might be in danger was unreal to me then.

But not for long.

8

I was the first one up the next morning. I'd been
lying awake anyway, thinking circles of thoughts
that wouldn't slow down and let me sleep. Having
the kitchen area to myself at breakfast was a small
luxury. I made Cream of Wheat and toast and was
done before Sherry and the others came out of the
dorm room.

I went outside and breathed in the freshness of the
morning as I walked toward the mare barn. If only
this were all there was to life, I thought sadly, just
caring for the horses and enjoying the beauty of the
place. If only I didn't have to be suspicious of
everyone around me.

Bobby trundled past with a barrow load of wet
bedding. Up even earlier than I was, I mused. His
hands were too full to wave, but he tossed his head
and grinned at me. Such a *nice* guy. I did not want
him to be part of anything crooked.

The Baysfield filly was pacing in her stall this
morning. Chris had said she was to be turned out in
the small paddock with two other weanlings this
morning, so I held her firmly by her tiny halter and
led her to the paddock. She bounced and jerked, and
I almost lost her once.

The paddock had five-foot-high plank fences,
smooth on the inner surface so that silly weanlings

couldn't hurt themselves. I stood just inside the latched gate and watched while the filly galloped around and around the enclosure, stirring the other foals to her own pitch of excitement.

From beyond the fence a mare whinnied, and the foal answered. In a flash of movement the filly threw herself at the top of the fence, clawed at it with her forelegs, then hung there, screaming.

I yelled, too, for any kind of help and ran to her. One foreleg was over the top board but tucked back into the fence, between the top and second boards.

Desperately I wrapped my arms around her body to ease the weight off that fragile leg. I gathered my breath to yell again, but Bobby was there suddenly.

His arm dived between me and the filly. He eased her against his own muscular body and raised his leg to support her, so that she was sitting on his knee. The cords in his neck bulged with the effort of supporting more than a hundred pounds of thrashing horse.

As swiftly as my shaking hands would move, I gripped the trapped hoof and pushed it outward through the fence. The freed leg slid over the fence top, and Bobby staggered backward. For an instant the three of us leaned toward each other. Then the foal bolted.

Bobby and I leaned unselfconsciously against each other, puffing and laughing a little. The filly stood with the other foals, sweating and trembling still but with full weight on the endangered leg.

"I can't believe she didn't break it," I panted. "Boy, was I glad to see you."

I looked up at him, and I knew. Whatever might have happened here, stable fires and switched stallions and all the rest of it, this good person had not hurt anyone, man or horse.

As I caught the filly and led her back to the barn for treatment of the scraped places on her leg, I told myself that although I was going to have to ask Bobby questions, I was no longer going to consider him a suspect. Not in my own mind, anyhow. He was a friend, and I refused to be *that* much of a detective.

Thursday evening was a typical evening in the dorm lounge. The TV was on, but no one was actually watching it. Randy and Bobby were playing a one-sided game of pool; most of the others were leafing through magazines, talking, laughing, or arguing. There was an ongoing harangue about whether to go into town or not. Someone wanted to price radial tires at the Sears store in the mall, someone else said, "Nah, you don't want to do that," and on and on.

I was watching JoJean and Amy slog their way through an incredibly slow game of Scrabble. They were the other two girls who shared the women's end of the dorm with Sherry and me. JoJean was pleasant enough, with a slow-moving sense of humor and a build like a quarterback. I guessed her to be in her early thirties. Amy was small and round and fluff-headed, sweet and funny and easily my favorite among the Wood Hill women, except, of course, for Chris, who was the person I hoped to be someday.

I watched over Amy's shoulder but shook my head when they tried to get me to play. I knew from unhappy experience back home that word games were a strong point of mine, and nobody likes a person who beats them all the time. I would wipe up the boards with opponents like Amy and JoJean, who for the past several minutes had been overlooking a chance for *oxen* that would have landed the X on a triple-score square and netted her thirty easy points.

So I sat on the arm of Amy's chair and watched and kept my mouth shut and thought about how to make the big disclosure that I was from Tradition Farm.

Sherry, whose absence had been commented on but not explained, came in from outside, glanced at me with a stiff face, and hurried through to our room, sketching a wave at the group with her hand but not saying anything.

Amy and I frowned at each other, puzzled, and JoJean said, "What's with her?"

From the pool table Randy said, "Come on, Bob, that's ten you owe me for this game, and five for last time."

One of the other men lifted his face from his magazine and said, "For Christ's sake, Bobby, quit playing pool with that shark while you've still got your gold fillings in your back teeth."

The outside door opened again, and Chris stuck her head in. She lived in her own separate log cabin, up a pine-needle path from the stable complex, and seldom came into the dorm.

"Gusty, see you a minute?" she called.

I shoved up from the chair arm, whispered in Amy's ear, "Try *havoc* down from *forth,*" and followed Chris out into the night.

"What's up?" I asked, but she said nothing, just opened the office door and nodded me through. Beneath what I hoped was a casual exterior my instincts bristled.

Chris walked behind her desk, but instead of sitting, she stood facing me, her features hard. She's having a rough time here, I realized with surprise.

"Gusty, I'm going to have to let you go."

"What? You mean, fire me?" For some reason I was totally unprepared for that. "Why? What did I do?"

Fleetingly I remembered Sherry skulking through the lounge just now. . . .

"You lied about your work history, for starters," Chris said. Her voice was flinty. "You told me this was your first job and that you were from Michigan. It's just come to my attention that you came here from Tradition Farm, not from Michigan, and I've just called the stable manager there to confirm. He also told me—"

"That he fired me for selling information," I rushed in, "but I didn't do it, Chris."

"I don't give a damn, Gusty. You lied. If you'd been straight with me when you applied for this job, I might have been willing to give you the benefit of the doubt about Mr. DeVrees's charges against you. I wouldn't have put you anywhere near the horses in training, maybe, but if you'd been honest . . ."

There was a personal quaver in her voice. This was something more to her than just firing an employee. She must have liked me, in the same way that I liked her. I saw in her what I hoped to be as I got older. Maybe she saw in me something of herself when she was starting out. Maybe that's why this was hurting her.

I opened my mouth to explain the whole situation to her . . . then shut it again. Someone in this place had conspired to steal a valuable horse and perpetrate a mammoth fraud on the breeding public. I didn't know that Chris wasn't a part of it. I liked her, and I didn't *think* she'd be involved; but I didn't actually know.

So I shut my mouth and swallowed the bitterness of allowing someone I respected to believe I was a liar. Or worse.

When this is all over, I promised myself, I want Chris to know what I was doing here.

I said, "How did you find out?"

"Sherry." Chris dropped wearily into her chair, and I sat, too, on the leather sofa along the wall. Above me was the win picture of American Express and all his smiling connections.

She went on. "Sherry happened to notice that your car's license plates were Ohio, not Michigan."

Damn. License plates. That was dumb of me.

"So she looked in through the back window and saw a cardboard box or something, with a mailing label that said 'Tradition Farm, Laurel, Ohio.' She came and told me. And she was right to," Chris added almost belligerently.

Cardboard box. The two big cartons in which I'd packed my clothes and books and personal odds and ends. One of the boxes had originally brought Pop my Christmas packages from Mom a few years ago. His name was on the label, along with the damning address.

So now Sherry, and possibly Chris, and possibly anyone else they talked to knew I was connected with Pop, as well as with Tradition Farm. And if someone here had had a hand in Pop's death because of something he might have learned or suspected about the stallion switch, then how safe was I?

Chris went on. "I'm sorry about this, Gusty. You've been an excellent worker, and you'd have been riding for us before long, I imagine. But a racing stable has to have security, as you know. We can't have employees who aren't a hundred percent trustworthy.''

The words burned against me like acid. Their hurting power surprised me. I knew why I was here. I knew I was honest. Still, I felt diminished by my reflection in Chris's eyes.

Chris got out the oversize ledger book that held the checks and began figuring my wages. She wrote the check and tore it out.

''Here, Gusty. This covers the week through today. You can leave first thing in the morning. Your reason for leaving is private as far as I'm concerned. You can tell the others whatever you like.''

I nodded, accepted the check, thought ruefully that severance checks were becoming a way of life for me.

We left the office, Chris going ahead of me through the door. I started to pull the heavy wooden door closed, then, on an impulse, eased up on the pull at the last second so that although the door closed, the tongue of the lock did not spring into place. Once sprung, the door would be locked until Chris opened it in the morning with her key. I had no clear idea in mind at that time, just an impulse, a feeling, that before the night was over, I might want access to the office records.

We stood in the moonlit driveway between office and dorm, facing each other awkwardly. ''I'm sorry about this,'' I said, and at the same time Chris said, ''I'm sorry, Gusty.''

We smiled ruefully and separated.

* * *

All conversations ceased in the lounge when I opened the door. Heads turned toward me, and suddenly new conversations sprang up like weeds after a rain. Sherry watched me from behind the curtain of her hair as she bent over the Scrabble board with JoJean and Amy. Amy stared at me openly, dismay and fascination equally obvious on her round little face.

I cleared my throat and said, "I'm going to go check that Baysfield filly again."

I went to the mare barn and looked in on the filly, who was asleep in her bedding. A few tears of self-pity stung through the bridge of my nose but got no farther than that. There was too much to think about, too much to do. I'd wallow later, I decided.

I turned off the light and stood against the barn wall, hoping that Bobby would be coming out, as he often did just before bedtime, apparently just to look at the stars or think his own private thoughts. Certainly I was in no hurry to go back in and face Sherry and the others in our communal bedroom.

After a while Bobby did come out, and he sat as usual on the log that separated lawn from parking area. I went over to him. "Bobby, come for a walk with me, will you?"

He looked up, surprised but pleased by the invitation. We walked slowly down the moonlit curve of the main drive, leading between fenced paddocks from the stable complex, past the owners' house and toward the highway.

"Did you lose a lot playing pool tonight?" I asked.

"Thirty dollars," Bobby said grimly.

"Why do you play with Randy if he takes your money like that?"

He shrugged his rounded shoulders, then said, "Sherry told us Chris was going to fire you. Did she fire you?"

"Yep."

"How come? Didn't you get all the wet places out of your stalls?" he asked sarcastically, and I wondered what hostility he might be feeling toward Randy, who was his immediate boss.

"No, she fired me because I lied to her when she hired me. I told her I hadn't worked in a stable before, but I had. I used to work at Tradition Farm, up in Ohio."

"Tradition Farm?" Bobby tilted his head to ponder. "I've heard of Tradition Farm."

"What did you hear about it?" I held my breath.

"I don't remember."

We walked in silence all the way out to the road, then turned and started back more slowly. I said, "Bobby, you told me you used to take care of Mutt, didn't you?"

"Yeah." He grinned ruefully. "He was the best horse I ever had."

"When he died, did they ask you to look at his body, to identify him?"

"Yeah," he said. "They took me up the mountain in a jeep." He waved toward the north.

"How long had Mutt been dead when you identified him?"

"How long?" He seemed confused by the question.

"How long after the fire was it when you identified him?"

"It was in the springtime, so it must have been a couple of months," he said firmly.

"When you identified him?"

He nodded.

"And the fire was a long time before that?"

"The fire was at Christmastime because they got mad at us for having decorations in the barns. They said maybe the Christmas decorations started the fire, but I don't think they did. We just put up some pine branches around the door, and I put the tinsel on and some little bells."

"Mutt must have been in pretty bad shape when you saw his body then, huh? It must have looked awful."

I was reminded of the old entertainers' trick of wiping a smile off with a sweep of a hand, leaving a frown in its place. Christmas and tinsel and bells were wiped away from Bobby's face and instantly replaced by reflected grimness of memory.

"You could see his bones in lots of places," he said in a low voice.

"But you knew for sure it was Mutt?"

"Well, I was going to look at his eye to see if the white spot was there, but his eye . . ." He looked sickened by his mental pictures.

"What white spot?" I prodded as gently as I could. This might be what I wanted.

"Mutt had a little teeny white spot on his eyeball, just teeny." He held up thumb and finger to show a sixteenth of an inch or so. "He poked his eye with a twig when he was a baby, chasing around the pasture. It didn't hurt his sight; it was just a spot there."

I nodded. One of the mares I'd ridden years ago had a similar white spot. Pop had explained it as a gathering of white cells at the injury site, nothing to worry about.

"Was that the only way you had to tell if it was really Mutt?" I asked.

"It was Mutt. He was a lighter color, I thought, but Randy said they get that way after they're dead. The sun fades them. But it was Mutt. He had his name on his halter."

I nodded. Excitement rose like a slow bubble. The horse on the mountain could very well have been a ringer. The identification was full of holes . . . and now I had something to take back, to check against Toby: a white spot on the eye.

"Randy," Bobby said suddenly.

"What?"

"That was what I was trying to think of a while ago. Randy was the one that told me about Tradition Farm. His uncle works there."

"Randy's uncle works at Tradition? What's his uncle's name?" My heart stopped.

But Bobby shook his head. "I don't know. You could ask Randy," he said, and again his voice became sharp-edged at the name, and I wondered about the two of them. If Randy was the bad apple at Wood Hill, my instinct told me Bobby could be counted on for help against him.

Randy must be the connection on this end. I grew excited. Randy was hungry for money for his health club, and he might very well have no scruples about where it came from. His conscience certainly had nothing to say about fleecing Bobby at the pool table. And if Randy knew how much I knew about him and he knew I was from Tradition . . .

I shivered in the chill of the thought.

9

Bobby went inside, but I stayed out, sitting on the lawn-edging log until every light was out in the dorm building, every radio silenced.

It was beautiful there, the tree-covered slope leading away toward higher hills to the south, the clear, star-pricked sky, the silent sturdy buildings with their soft sounds of rustling bedding, snuffling muzzles. A foal whinnied, and its mother, in another paddock, answered.

I would have pangs leaving this place, I thought. Nothing like the wrench of leaving Tradition, which was, after all, my home, but pangs all the same.

No time to wallow in that now, though. My mind was on that office door, incompletely closed. Within the office were employment files, and somewhere in there were Randy's home address and parents' names.

Randy's last name didn't match anyone's at Tradition, at least no one I knew. But an uncle could be his mother's brother, different last name. The connection might be found if I dropped in for a visit at his home. On what excuse? I'd have to think of one.

Then, with Randy as the logical connection on this end, and a relative of his at Tradition, and the laughably shaky identification of American Express to add to the bits and pieces that had sent me here in the first place, I should have enough to go to someone in authority, police or Jockey Club or someone better able than I was to get into the heavy slugging.

It was after midnight before I felt safe in approaching the office, and then "safe" was stretching it a mountain mile. Glancing around, I detoured to the mare barn. I had an excuse to be there if I came upon anyone: I was checking on the filly.

Just inside the door, on a cross brace two-by-four, stood a silver flashlight. I tested it and found the light weak but better than nothing. I dropped it down my shirtfront since there were no pockets in my jeans loose enough to hold it. It rode cold and ridiculous against my stomach.

Nothing stirred in the stable area. Holding my breath, I moved in the moon shadows against the mare barn, under the trees, finally along the office wall. So far, so good.

The door gave under my hand, and I was inside. Quickly I pushed the door shut and groped my way around the desk to the file cabinet. I was afraid to turn on the flashlight for fear someone outside would see it.

I pulled open the top file drawer, easing it on its potentially squeaky track. Nosing the flashlight well down into the drawer, I snapped it on. The beam illuminated the file folders' labels. "Receipts Hay," "Receipts Grain," "Receipts Farrier," "Receipts Veterinary" . . .

Deep in the drawer I found a file marked "Employment Applications." Ah. I pulled out the file folder and opened it. Holding the flashlight under my chin now, I leafed quickly through. My nerves twanged with flight instinct. Get out while it's safe! Quick! Quick!

I don't have the nerves for this business, I thought fleetingly.

And there it was. Randy Welch. Home address, Route 1, Box 315, Fincastle, Ohio. Parents, Richard and Norma Welch, same address. I glanced through the application form, saw nothing else important, and closed the file. "Richard and Norma Welch, Fincastle, Ohio," I recited.

Light off, I felt my way around the desk, peered out through the door, and slipped out, pulling it shut hard behind me. Ah! Whew.

Feeling giddy with relief and excitement, I started toward the dorm.

Suddenly there was a whoosh of movement behind me, an arm clamped hard against my throat. My head jerked back. I tried to scream, to gasp, but bug-eyed, I found I couldn't even breathe.

I was dragged backward, my heels scraping foolishly across the grass. I thrashed my arms, struck out with the flashlight, which was still in my hand, but I could grasp nothing, hit nothing.

Trees passed my face. We were in the dense grove of pine and pin oak behind the dorm, a place too tangled for the mowing machine to penetrate.

Real fear froze me. This was too isolated a spot.

The man smothered my face with his hand, smashing my nose, jabbing his thumb against the side of my eyeball. I went weak and still with terror, as a rabbit does in the grip of the dog.

A voice whispered roughly against my hair. "Listen, you. You get out of here and you mind your own business, you hear me?"

I didn't move.

"You hear me?" The arm around my throat jerked back, mashing my windpipe. Terrified, I moved my head in a nodding motion against his chest. As my eyes widened, I saw in the corner of my vision a strand of wavy blond hair.

It was Randy. Of course, it was Randy.

Somehow knowing that it was Randy lightened my fear. I couldn't imagine that a boy I knew, a boy who hustled poor Bobby out of pool bets, was really going to kill me in the woods. It was possible, but it was also somehow absurd.

When his arm loosened enough for speech, I said, with all the dignity I could muster, "Come on, Randy, grow up."

It was a mistake. He became rigid against my back, his arm again a steel vise against my throat. My ears began to ring, and pinwheels of light spun behind my eyes.

"Bitch," he breathed. He spun me around and drove his fist into my stomach. The pain was beyond bearing. I bent double around it, sank toward the ground. Something crashed against the back of my neck.

I collapsed. Moist, moldy leaves brushed against my face, wet earth against my nose. There was one last explosion of pain, a full-force kick aimed at my stomach but blocked by my updrawn legs. He arched over my head, then disappeared into blackness.

At least I'm still alive.

That thought was the first clear one that came up through the swirling pain as I surfaced to consciousness.

My face was still half buried in a crust of last

year's leaves and pine needles. I began drawing up my knees, trying to get up. Pain roared through me, making my head swim, my eyes water.

The great temptation at that moment was to sink back into the mattress of leaves, just to lie there until some kind person found me and called an ambulance.

But what if it weren't a kind person who found me? What if Randy had just grabbed me on impulse when he saw me come out of the office, thinking he'd beat me up as a scare tactic? And then suppose he had second thoughts and decided to come back. He might decide he had too much at stake to leave me alive.

That possibility injected strength into my screaming muscles, and I pulled myself up to hands and knees.

Somewhere behind me a twig snapped. Terror shot through me. Forcing my hands to move and my legs to follow, I crawled around the base of a fat oak tree, getting it between me and the place I'd fallen. If he was coming back, looking for me . . .

My right leg didn't seem to work. I could drag it forward by pendulum action, just far enough to support my weight on it, but couldn't swing it under my body for forward progress. I crawled on in hip-hop fashion anyway, hearing rustling, snapping sounds, like footsteps.

Another tree between me and my previous bed. Slowly, painfully, another tree and another. I was going in a zigzag pattern now, more from dizziness than shrewdness.

It occurred to me that I was probably going deeper into the woods, farther from the safety of the dorm and other people. If he was coming after me, this was the worst thing I could do.

I rolled over into a sitting position with my back against a tree trunk. My vision was clearing by now, although I seemed to have the use of only my left eye. I put my hand up and found a deep bleeding gash above my right eye; the eye was crusted shut with dirt and leaves and drying blood.

Cautiously I reached above my head for a low tree branch and used it to pull myself by gradual stages to my feet. My right leg folded under my weight, and only the tree kept me upright. My stomach surged. Abruptly I sank to my knees and leaned over to rid myself of supper.

Spitting weakly, fighting tears, I got to my feet again and tried to find a sense of direction. I felt that the buildings were ahead of me and to my left, but since I couldn't actually see anything but trees and bushes, all dimly outlined by moonlight, I couldn't be sure.

I tested my right leg again. It was deadened but apparently not broken since there was no new pain when I put weight on it. The bones all seemed to be aligned about right. I thanked heaven that the taped ankle had healed as quickly from the riding accident as it had and was back to full strength since that was my only good leg at the moment.

I tried to remember the geography of the woods but had to give it up. In the week that I'd been here, all my time had been spent around the stable complex or in the mares' pasture on the far side of the buildings. All I knew about this patch of woods was what could be seen from the dorm windows, and I'd spent very little time looking out of them. It might be a shallow belt of woods opening to pasture or hayfield, or it might go on for miles, back toward the higher mountains where the dead horse had been found.

I wondered if a man who had killed a horse to further a switch scheme would also be capable of killing, and willing to kill, a human being?

Suddenly I tensed. There *were* noises in the woods, a snap, a pause, another muffled shuffled, snapping sound, another pause. I stared in the direction of the sounds, which, I thought, was also the direction of the buildings.

In a space between trees he was suddenly there, a hulking shape walking slowly, turning his head from side to side so that the moonlight glinted from his long blond curls. In the faint light I could just make out something—a coil of rope?—over his shoulder.

In a fluid motion I faded back behind the tree, drawing in my arms and flattening myself against the terrifyingly narrow trunk. My breath stopped; my heart pounded on. I could feel it hammering in my throat.

Step . . . pause . . . step. Getting closer? Going past? I couldn't tell.

My legs trembled with the effort of holding me up, pressing me against the tree. I had an almost overwhelming urge to scream, to jump out and wave my arms at him, get it over with. The tension was unbearable.

Seconds passed, a full minute. The crunch of the footsteps seemed to have stopped, but my pulse was pounding so loudly in my ears that I wasn't sure.

Finally, steeling myself, I turned my head and eased it around the trunk. The space where I had seen him was empty. I moved my head farther.

There was nothing in the woods, no man, no coiled rope.

Listening, listening, I moved forward toward the spot where I had seen him. The ground was clear of underbrush there. I looked to the left and right and decided it was a path. Take it? Stay in the cover of the brush? I had to decide and suddenly couldn't. It was all too much. I was sick and exhausted, and I really did not want any of this.

The path was probably the easiest and fastest way back to the buildings. It was also the place he was most likely to reappear if he searched awhile and decided to come back.

I pulled myself into the woods beyond the path and began working my way forward and to the left, in a course roughly parallel to where I imagined the path to be, but several yards left of it, where the screen of berry bushes and pine seedlings hid me.

It was almost impossible to move silently while dragging my right foot, but I did my best. I supported myself from one handhold to the next on whatever trees lent themselves to the purpose.

I leaned on a sapling, and it broke beneath my weight; it was not a sapling at all but a dead branch blown down from an oak tree and caught in an upright position by its branches. It sent a gunshot crack echoing through the woods.

Damn.

I moved faster, knowing that if he was in the woods, he must have heard that crack and was probably doubling back, following the sound.

I got into a dead end, a horseshoe of blackberry bushes too dense and thorny to push through. Backing up, circling, I fought a desire to weep.

Suddenly there was a light shining through the

trees ahead and, to my right, a high blue-white light, the most beautiful light I'd ever seen.

The security light at the stable complex.

I moved forward faster now, hobbling with some weight on my right foot. If it hurt, I didn't notice. There before me, under the security light, stood my most beloved friend. The VW Bug.

Without its keys.

Keys. Damn. Inside the dorm, in my purse.

Oh well, I sighed, I'd have to get the purse anyway. It held every penny I owned.

Scanning the area carefully, I stepped out of the sheltering bushes and half ran toward the dorm. As I bolted for the door, a movement beyond the corner of the building caught my eye.

Randy.

He was emerging from the woods path, the coil of rope still over his shoulder. I couldn't tell whether he'd seen me or not, but at least there were other people here.

I eased through the front door and felt my way around sofa and pool table and into the women's room. Sherry, Amy, and JoJean were mounds in their beds.

I looked at my own bed. So tempting. Safe? Probably. Just lie down there under that plaid spread and green cotton blanket, lie there until the safe light of morning, and then drive away.

But I looked through the window toward the woods, and saw a movement there, and decided no. No lying down, no closing eyes. Not in this place.

I reached into the space under my nightstand and got my purse. Then I hesitated. All I had in this room was a nylon weekend bag, a few pairs of underwear, my other jeans, and a few shirts and T-shirts. One sweater, a couple of pairs of socks. Not much. But they were mine, and he wasn't going to do me out of them.

Slowly, because my arm muscles weren't working very well, I fished the bag out of the closet at the end of the room and began laying in the clothes. Metal hangers rang against each other. I didn't much care.

Bag in one hand, purse slung over my shoulder, I maneuvered through the dark lounge and opened the front door.

He was waiting.

Six feet away, between me and the car, he stood facing me, his feet splayed in fighting stance, the rope in his two hands.

His face was hidden by moon shadow so that only the tip of his nose showed, and a wet line on the curve of his lip.

He was smiling.

Suddenly I was mad. Fury surged through me. I leaped toward him, swinging the weekend bag in a wild arc toward his head.

It was made of soft nylon and held only clothes; but he wasn't expecting the lunge, and it was powered by temporary insanity. Caught off-balance, he teetered back and stumbled on the lawn log, flinging his arms into the air.

By the time he hit the ground I was at the car. The door was unlocked, thank God. I threw the bag into the back and scrambled in, plunging my hand into the purse for the keys.

Billfold, pencils, wads of paper—where were the damned keys?

He was on his feet again and coming toward the car.

Frantically I bore down on the horn with one hand and went on scrabbling through my purse with the other.

Keys! Whew.

A light came on in the dorm.

I got the key into the ignition. Upside down.

He reached for the car door. I slammed down the lock button and jammed the key in again. The dorm door opened, and a man appeared.

Randy pounded on the car, rocking it. He looked insane.

The engine roared. I threw the shift into reverse and spun away, knocking him over again. Shift gears, lean on the gas, spin out over the gravel.

In the mirror I could see him getting up.

He had a car, a rust-spotted old Plymouth with one turquoise fender, but usually it was being taken apart for one reason or another. Was it running now? Could he follow me? I didn't know.

I was relieved to find that I could drive, but my right foot wasn't working very well. As soon as the car was up into high gear, I shifted feet and drove with my left.

The road was dark and twisty, and my one-eyed vision gave me no depth perception, so that I went into the curves without knowing precisely when to start my turns. I couldn't drive very far this way, I realized.

Nothing showed in the rearview mirror, no headlights catching up.

The narrow road gave out finally onto Highway 62, and I turned left, heading instinctively toward the lights of Cynthiana several miles away.

On the straighter road the driving was a little easier. When the town finally appeared, I stopped at

90

an all-night convenience store and gas station and hobbled into the rest room. I cleaned myself up as best I could, getting off the blood and dirt, anyway. Then, following directions from the cashier, I found the Rest Easy Motel.

It was on a side street half a block from the highway, and it was a small, shabby place lit only by a neon vacancy sign. It was a low frame structure, just one wing of rooms, painted a flamingo peach, or so it looked in the dark.

A woman in hair rollers and a quilted bathrobe took my money and handed over the maroon plastic tag and room key. Seventeen dollars. If she wondered about my cut forehead and overall awfulness of appearance, she said nothing. Apparently it was that kind of motel.

I drove the car around to the alley side of the building so it would be invisible to anyone cruising along, looking for me. Then, ignoring the suitcase and taking only my purse, I dragged myself those last long steps into my haven. I locked both locks and fastened the chain, pried off my shoes, and crawled into bed, jeans and shirt and all. I didn't give a damn about anything except oblivion.

10

A lifelong habit of waking when the sky lightened brought me out of my sleep. My watch said seven-thirty.

I lay back, moving various parts against the sheets to see how bad it was this morning. I could wiggle my right foot up and down, tenting up the blanket with no unbearable pain from the leg above it. Better than last night. And my vision seemed normal. Arms and hands moved all right, with stiffness and soreness in the muscles but nothing unbearable. It felt like the kind of stiffness that gets better with exercise.

I sat up. My midsection was the worst. I felt as though every organ inside me were bruised along with all the muscles that held me upright in the bed. Frowning, concerned now, I eased out of bed and went to the bathroom. Whew. No blood in my urine. Kidneys must not be damaged in any serious way.

I hobbled out to the car for my bag, then took a full-size bath, scrubbed my hair, put on clean stuff from the skin out, and felt much better.

First, a stop at the local bank to cash my severance check from Wood Hill, then a quick stop at the drugstore for a bandage for my forehead. I got a tin box of them, the largest size they had, and wondered ruefully if I was going to need the whole boxful before I was finished with this business.

There was no sign of an old Plymouth with a turquoise fender as I drove out onto the highway, but I still felt too close to Wood Hill to relax completely. Driving was comfortable, and I wasn't hungry yet, so I drove north to Cincinnati and beyond before I stopped at a Mister Donut for hot chocolate with whipped cream on top and a pair of cinnamon sugars.

Sitting on the counter stool, bending forward to shower my napkin with doughnut crumbs and cinnamon, I made my plans.

I could find some authorities to dump all this onto now while my wounds and bruises were convincing. I could go back to Tradition and see if Toby had a white spot on one eye, which would strengthen my story quite a bit when I did tell it to someone. Or I could go on up to Fincastle, find Randy's parents, try to find out what I could there before Randy got to them and possibly cut off that source of information. What could I learn from his parents? The name of his relative at Tradition, mainly.

That seemed worth the effort. I decided, after unfolding my Ohio road map on the Mister Donut counter and studying it, that I would drive east to Fincastle, about an hour, hour and a half from where I was on the outskirts of Cincinnati. I'd drop in on the Welches on some excuse, visit awhile, then drive back this way and get a motel room near Tradition. Then tonight try for a look at Toby, and first thing in the morning give it all to the authorities. After that . . .

I couldn't think past that.

* * *

"Mrs. Welch?"

"Yeah?" She was big and blond and had probably been pretty twenty years ago. She wouldn't be bad now except that her jeans and blouse were too tight, outlining the bulges of flesh around her underwear. Her hair was aggressively yellow. It didn't go with the soft-featured face and the farm wife backdrop. She looked as though she had spent her pretty girlhood playing the role of beautiful farmer's daughter and hadn't updated the role as her looks left her.

But her face was open and welcoming, and she held the screen door wide. It was a smallish farmhouse a few miles outside Fincastle. The gas station man had directed me to it easily. The house was small and square, the kind of house that had started life as farmhand quarters rather than owners' house.

"Do you have a son, Randy, who works in a Thoroughbred stable?" I asked, trying to remember my role.

"Sure. You a friend of his? Come on in, we're letting in the flies here."

I stepped through a service porch cluttered with deep-freeze and mud boots and cats and followed Mrs. Welch into the kitchen. It was big and busy-looking and decorated mostly in yellow linoleum.

"Have a sit," she said, waving me toward the kitchen table. "Coffee?"

"No, thanks."

She got herself a cup, swept aside a cereal bowl with cornflakes sticking to its sides, and sat down catercornered from me. Her face was still openly smiling. "Now then, what can I do for you?"

94

"Well, see, what it is, I'm a stable worker, too, and some of us have been talking about getting some kind of organization behind us, you know, not a labor union or anything like that, but just some kind of association that we could take problems to about wages and working hours and all that. Stable workers have no kind of protection at all, see."

Her expression politely urged me on, but I stole a moment to look around. I didn't see any family photographs, but then, we were in the kitchen. And nothing in Mrs. Welch's face gave me any clues either. If it was her brother working at Tradition, they must not look much alike. Probably her hair was dyed, for one thing.

I went on. "So I was wondering if you could tell me where Randy is working now, so I could get hold of him."

"Sure. He works for a place called Wood Hill Farm, and the address is Route Two, Cynthiana, Kentucky." Then, slightly puzzled, she said, "But how do you know Randy? Where did you know him from, to come looking for him?"

"Uh, a friend of mine gave me his name. She said they used to work together somewhere, but I didn't remember where. See, she just gave me a list of names of everybody she worked with at all the different places she worked. She job-hopped a lot," I finished confidently.

Mrs. Welch leaned back in her chair and fixed me with a dubious stare, and I suddenly felt that this woman was probably nobody's fool.

She stared, and I began to turn red. My eyes lowered to the tablecloth.

"Okay, honey," she said, "now you want to tell

me why you really came here? I didn't just fall off the turnip truck, you know."

I said nothing, blushed harder, and thought fast.

She chuckled. When I looked up, she was grinning at me in a way I can only describe as motherly.

"You know my Randy," she teased, "and you've got a crush on him, don't you?"

I smiled back, and my insides sank in relief. "Yeah," I admitted. "I work with Randy down at Wood Hill, and see, this is going to sound so silly, I hate to admit it . . ."

"You were curious to see his home and meet his folks." She finished for me.

I lowered my head again so she couldn't read my expression. "Yeah, something like that. But listen, please don't tell him I was here, okay? See, he's not interested in me at all, and I don't want him to think I'm chasing him or anything like that."

She patted my arm and stood up. "Honey, you don't need to worry about me. I think you're sweet, and I wish that boy would start paying attention to a nice little girl like you. What happened to your head there?"

I touched the bandage. "Accident."

"Horse kick you?"

"Yeah. Something like that. A jackass actually."

"They got a pet donkey at Wood Hill?"

"Yeah." I got off the subject. I didn't trust my sense of humor or her ability to pick up on double meanings. I stood up and looked around.

"Come on," she said, standing, too. "As long as you made the trip, I might as well show you around. This is the living room."

Obviously.

"And this in here is Randy's room. He don't come home very often anymore, but we keep it up for him anyway."

A small room, linoleum floor with a cheap rag rug, a narrow bed with a cowboy on a rearing horse on the spread. No books, no pictures or trophies, just a small plastic radio on an end table. I tried to visualize the little boy who had lived here, tried to superimpose that image over last night's horror stalking me through the woods, stalking with a rope over his shoulder. . . . I shuddered. I didn't know how his mother interpreted the shudder—sexual delight looking at my beloved's bedroom? Another shiver chased through me, and I turned away.

We walked back into the living room. It was a small, square room, furniture arranged flat against the walls. On the television set stood a cluster of photographs in cheap plastic or cardboard frames. I went over to them.

There were the usual boyhood pictures of Randy, small school photos showing a progression of lost teeth and shaved-off haircuts. There was also a snapshot of a young blond woman on a standing horse. I picked it up.

She was wearing western pants and shirt, not as fancy as Mrs. Jewett's, but the shirt looked satiny in the picture. The horse was a pinto in western tack.

"This is you?"

Her voice warmed. "That was me on Patootie. I got that horse when I was fourteen, and I kept him for eleven years, right through getting married and having Randy. Randy learned to ride on Patootie, matter of fact. God, how I bawled when that old horse finally died. My husband said he reckoned I wouldn't mourn that hard if he kicked the bucket himself, and he's probably more than half right."

"Do you still ride?" I asked with elaborate casualness.

"Oh, haven't much these last years. I did have an old horse for a while after Patootie died, old brown Standardbred, retired harness racer that my neighbor's nephew owned and kept here after they quit racing him. I used to ride him around the farm every little now and then, but he wasn't much of a pleasure horse, just between you and me. Hard-mouthed bastard, and he had a trot that'd shake your fillings loose."

"What happened to him?" I held my breath.

"Broke his leg. Had to be shot. Randy was home that weekend, luckily. Fact, Randy was riding him when he fell and broke the leg. I never did even see him. Randy hauled him off for me, so I didn't have to see him. Randy can be an awful sweet boy sometimes."

"Yeah."

It all fit. It fit perfectly.

The Standardbred would have been the horse on the mountain. Standardbreds were very often dark brown or brown-black, with little or no white on them. Randy would have known about the horse when all this was being planned. Not too hard then for him to come home for a visit at about the time when the switch was planned, take the horse out for a ride, load him up, and haul him away.

He had probably scouted the mountainous area behind Wood Hill, found some old jeep road, taken the Standardbred up there, and killed him in some hidden ravine where the body wouldn't be discovered until it had had time to decompose beyond certain identification. A switch of halters, and presto . . .

I asked, "Was that the last horse you had then? You don't have any now?"

"No, we haven't had any horses for five or six years now. My husband and me, we used to belong to the Saddle Club here in town, used to go on the trail rides when they had them. But then he bunged up his back and couldn't ride anymore, and I never liked to go without him. When Randy was little, we always had ponies for him, course. We all used to go out on family trail rides a lot, back in them years. That little Randy, he was such a scoot. He wasn't afraid of anything, I tell you. He'd get up on his dad's big old quarter horse and have that thing turning handstands for him practically. He was so cute."

I managed a fatuous smile, as a girl with a crush on Randy would have had at that point in the conversation.

"Did you have any other horses after the Standardbred, though?" I asked, rather more pointedly than was probably safe, but I needed to know.

"No."

My hopes sank.

"Only that one," she went on, remembering. "He wasn't here very long. Randy picked him up for me at a horse sale. He'd felt so bad, you know, about the accident with the Standardbred, even though that horse's owners were just as glad not to have to go on paying board for him. Randy offered to pay them for Mike—that was the Standardbred—but they didn't want nothing for him, just told Randy to forget it. But still, he felt bad, you know."

I nodded. I knew all about Randy's kind heart.

My bruised arms and thigh and belly knew all about Randy's kind heart.

"So he brought you another horse?" I prodded casually.

"Yes, well, he picked this one up at some sale somewhere, but we didn't have him very long. He was a stallion. I was all for having him gelded, but Randy found out I was going to do it and threw one of his little temper tantrums." She smiled a mother's indulgent smile, and I answered with a crooked one of my own.

Little temper tantrums. Yes, indeed. I could imagine how Randy might have reacted to his mother's announcement that American Express was about to be gelded.

"Was he a nice riding horse?" I asked.

"Well, not at first. He'd had surgery in his mouth, had some warts removed up under his lip, the way Randy told it. So he couldn't wear a bridle with a bit; but I tried him with my old hackamore, and he went pretty well in that. He was an awful fast horse, though. Ran away with me a couple of times. My husband, he didn't like me riding him. We thought if we had him gelded, that would settle him down, but Randy threw a fit about it. So we just quit graining him, turned him out on pasture, and after a while he settled down into a nice riding horse."

"So what happened to him?" Again I held my breath.

"My uncle bought him off me. He works at a stable, too, down by Cincinnati, and the lady that owned the place was looking for a nice classy saddle horse, and from what my uncle said, she wanted a stallion. You know how some people are, they like the idea of riding a stallion. So he bought that horse off me for his boss. I didn't really care. You get on my side of forty, honey, and you kind of lose interest in all that stuff.''

I nodded. This was it. I had it now. Just one more crucial thing, and I could get out of here.

"I used to work at a stable near Cincinnati myself. Tradition Farm. That wouldn't have been where your uncle is, I suppose?''

I deserved an Oscar for this.

Her face lit. "Yes, Tradition Farm. You probably knew him then. His name is— Now who could that be?''

A car door slammed beyond the open window, and heavy feet pounded on the porch steps.

"Ma," he bellowed.

I froze.

11

"Look who's here," Mrs. Welch said brightly. I didn't know which of us she was talking about. Randy and I stared at each other across the living room, eyes locked like a snake and a mongoose just before the death strike.

"What's she doing here?" Randy said finally to his mother, although his eyes never left mine.

"Now, Randy"—the woman's voice soothed and humored him—"don't get your back up, honey. I like this little girl. She likes you, and she just wanted a look at your home and family. Nothing wrong with that now, is there? What are you doing home on a Friday? Do you have a day off, or what?"

His eyes bored into mine. "What have you been talking about?" His voice was so thick with fury that his mother looked at him oddly.

I smiled and shrugged. "Like she said, I just wanted to see where you lived. You know I've got this thing for you," I admitted, lowering my eyes and voice and trying to blush.

He did a quick double take.

"Well," I said briskly, "this is kind of embarrassing, so I believe I'll just be on my way." I edged toward the door.

He moved toward me, hesitated, looked at his mother. He seemed at a loss.

I darted through the kitchen and out the door.

"Nice meeting you, honey," Mrs. Welch called after me. "Now you come back and visit me when you're in the neighborhood, hear?"

"Thanks. Bye."

I bolted for the car. Through the open window I heard him bellow, "What did you tell her? What were you talking about?"

I drove away, shaking.

Had he followed me after all? Or had he come up here on the run, not knowing how much I knew or guessed about the stallion switch and wanting to warn his mother not to tell anyone about Toby, who had obviously been the stallion at the farm those few months, recovering from mouth surgery.

I turned off the highway and wove through gravel roads, turning right, then left, then right, at the mile squares. I was positive he wasn't following me, but I couldn't seem to stop dodging.

It was three o'clock by the time I emerged onto pavement and headed south. I pulled off onto the shoulder, located myself on the road map, and set a course south and west toward Tradition Farm. Although I wasn't hungry, I stopped at a McDonald's in Georgetown and forced down a hamburger, my only food all day except for the two doughnuts years ago that morning.

As I drove, I sorted.

Things seemed fairly clear on the Kentucky end of the business now. I tried to backtrack and figure out how the whole thing got started, how it had worked.

Mrs. Welch's uncle—that would be Randy's great-uncle actually, whose name I'd missed by a maddening split second—worked at Tradition and probably came up with the plan, maybe after visiting Randy at Wood Hill and seeing American Express and his colts. Great-uncle and nephew might have talked casually about Ambassador and his worthless colts, ruefully comparing them to American Express. Someone might have said, "If only they could trade places . . ."

But why? Why would these two men stick their necks out to the extent of staging a barn fire, planting the Standardbred on the mountain, making off with American Express during the fire confusion and hiding him at the Welch farm, then shuttling him on to Tradition, having probably also engineered the colic death of old Trigger to create a need for American Express, aka Toby?

There had to be a huge profit motive in this somewhere. I could see Randy doing almost anything, including starting fires and killing horses. It would have been hard for me to believe before last night's attack in the woods, but now I could imagine him doing things like that, especially if it meant a big chunk of money toward his health club.

Okay, so that was Randy's part. What about the unnamed uncle at Tradition? Who could it be? I wouldn't have suspected Randy with his long blond curls of being that kind of person. Who else did I know that I hadn't thought capable of this kind of thing? Who at Tradition?

One thing I did know, and that knowledge grew with the miles speeding past.

I was now in danger. Genuine danger.

Randy would have found out by now that his

mother had chatted to me about the horses. He knew that I'd already known or guessed enough to send me there asking questions. I was dangerous to Randy and to whoever was at Tradition.

And therefore, Randy was dangerous to me. He had beaten me badly last night, had left me unconscious, and had come back to find me with a rope. Why? To tie me up and haul me away into the mountains? Remembering Bobby's description of the carcass of the horse, I shuddered. A girl's body would be easy to hide in those rocky, forested slopes. Easier than a horse.

Okay, McCaw, I thought, time to turn this over to somebody else.

I drove past the turnoff to Laurel and Tradition and kept on toward Cincinnati until the anonymity of the city's outskirts grew around me. Then an overwhelming weariness weakened my grip on the steering wheel, and I turned in at a large Holiday Inn.

My room was big, all bright blues and greens with a balcony that opened onto the swimming pool. There was a basket of fancy souvenirs on the lavatory: shampoo and face soap and shower cap and cologne. Nice.

I flopped on the bed and lay spread-eagle, wishing I were there on a carefree vacation trip with nothing more to worry about than messing up my hairdo in the pool before dinner.

Exhaustion weakened me emotionally as well as physically, and I gave in to a wave of loneliness worse than any that had hit me since Pop died. I needed somebody to talk to about all this. I needed somebody whose shoulder I could bury my face in, who would stroke my hair and say: "There, there now, Gusty, everything's going to be all right."

For a mad moment I pictured myself leaning into the motherly warmth of Mrs. Welch. She was wasted on Randy, that bastard. Why couldn't I wallow in a little of that mother love?

Instead, I had to drag myself back into the mess at hand. It was four-thirty. If I were going to call someone, I'd better get to it.

Okay. Who? Police? Jockey Club? It had an office in Lexington, not too far from here, and I knew, in the general way that such knowledge is picked up around a stable, that the Jockey Club had a security division that policed things like frauds and ringers and shady doings in the world of Thoroughbred racing.

Probably the local police at Cynthiana would be more logical, I thought. I could report Randy's beating last night, and I could tell them what I suspected about the horses. They would probably pick Randy up for the beating he gave me, look into the horse thing, but would they have the specific knowledge necessary to sort out the ramifications of the stallion switch? Maybe, maybe not. And how long could they keep him safely locked up on only an assault charge?

Would they believe me? Maybe, maybe not.

Or I could call the Jockey Club. . . . Yes. That idea was somehow more comfortable. The Jockey Club would be horse people. I could talk to them more easily than to police.

I sat up on the bed and picked up the phone. It took me a while to figure out which buttons to punch for an outside long-distance line, but eventually I got

Directory Assistance, got the Jockey Club number in Lexington, and dialed.

"Could I talk to someone in your security division?" I asked.

"That would be Mr. Penn. I'll ring."

So far so good.

"Theo Penn, may I help you?" The man recited the words but sounded as though his mind were elsewhere. Almost five o'clock on a Friday afternoon. I felt as though I must rush to get my story in before he left for the weekend.

"Mr. Penn?"

"Yes, may I help you?" He sounded faintly impatient.

"Um, my name is Augusta McCaw? I work at Wood Hill Farm at Cynthiana? Or rather, I used to, um, I used to work at Tradition Farm at Laurel, Ohio?"

"Yes?" Now he sounded slightly more interested.

"Well, Mr. Penn, I don't exactly know how to explain this, but I think that American Express . . . you remember him?"

"Yes. Of course. Died in a stable fire six, seven years ago."

"Yes. No, actually, I don't believe he did. I think he's at Tradition Farm now, but under a different name, and I think he's being used at stud under Ambassador's name."

There was a very long pause.

"Mr. Penn?"

"Yes. I'm here. Give me your name again."

"Augusta McCaw. Gusty." I spelled it for him. Lots of people thought it was McCall, just hearing it.

"Yes, all right, Gusty. Gusty? How old are you, young lady?"

I bristled. "What's that got to do with it?"

"Well now, you're making some pretty serious accusations here, Miss McCaw, and just a bit farfetched. I think I have a right to find out if you know what you're talking about."

"I'm seventeen," I said wearily.

He didn't reply. I had the feeling that he was making a note of the damning fact that I was only seventeen or possibly that he was tearing up his previous notes and deciding not to bother.

"Look," I snapped, "I got beat up pretty badly last night by the jerk that set that fire and stole American Express and killed the poor Standardbred up on the mountain, and I've got one hell of a stomachache, not to mention a face that I probably should have got stitches in except I was too busy hiding from him, and if you're not going to take me seriously about this, then . . ." I was too close to tears to think of an adequate threat.

"Where are you calling from, Miss McCaw?" His voice was soothing now. Humoring the crazy kid.

"I'm at a Holiday Inn, I don't know, someplace on the east side of Cincinnati, on Fifty-two. Now are you going to help me with this, or what?"

"I'll certainly look into the situation, Miss McCaw. Now if you would just tell me why it is that you have these suspicions, we can go from there."

Pulling in a big breath, I started with my discovery of the midnight breeding a week ago, backtracked to Pop's death, then worked my way forward through what I'd learned at Wood Hill and at Randy's parents' farm.

When finally the story wound down, I took in another long breath and waited for the reaction from the other end of the line.

"Um. Um, um, um," he muttered.

"What does that mean?" I snapped. I was perched on the edge of the bed, trembling with the need for an ally in this frightening business, and all he could say was "um, um."

Mr. Penn said doubtfully, "Well, Miss McCaw, your theory . . ."

"Look, buster," I yelled, "this gash on my face is not theoretical. And you should see my stomach and my thigh. If you think I'm some hysterical kid just making this up, to hell with you. I need some help here. I don't need some desk jockey telling me I'm hysterical."

I slammed down the phone. Hysterically.

Cursing under my breath with all the foul words a lifetime in the stable had netted me, I grabbed my purse and slammed out of the room. If he called back, I didn't want to be there.

Dimly I knew I was being unreasonable. The man had a right to question me. I knew that I knew what I knew, but he didn't have anything to go on except for what little I, a stranger . . . and seventeen . . . had just told him.

I slumped into a small booth in the coffee shop, ordered a Coke as the price for sitting there, and tried to think logically. Logically, I should go back up to my room, call the poor guy back and apologize, see whether or not he intended to do anything about the situation, and then take a nice soaking bath and crawl into that bed.

But logically or not, my feathers were still ruffled. It was infuriating that after all I'd been through this past week, the first question out of his mouth had been: "How old are you?"

Just theory, he said. Well, in a way that was true, but the facts were there, too: Randy's attack on me, his warning to his mother, the Standardbred and his oh-so-convenient death . . . all kinds of little facts that dovetailed into an almost complete picture. There just wasn't hard evidence yet.

Okay, if he wanted proof, he would damn well have it.

The spot on Toby's eye.

Beyond the entrance to Tradition Farm was a belt of woods, and beyond the woods a flat open area held the training track, a three-quarter-mile oval fenced in by white boards with a smaller track inside it. From the main road a dirt service road led back to the track area. It was used mostly by the tractors that groomed the track and by visitors driving in to watch the workouts. I turned into the service road and cut the headlights.

It was just past midnight. I'd rested in my room, even dozing a little, until it was late enough to start out for Tradition. I'd tried to call back the Jockey Club man to apologize, but no one answered. Through the naptime my courage had begun to slip, and by the time I left the shelter of the Holiday Inn I'd begun wishing deeply that I didn't have to do this. Again, a small flame of anger toward Mr. Penn for abandoning me in this mess had burned in me, and I recommitted myself to going through with the trip to Tradition.

The moon wasn't nearly as full and helpful as it

had been the previous week. If I hadn't been familiar with the service road, I'd have been afraid to nose the car along its almost invisible path. On my left the dense blackness of the woods; on my right I could dimly see the oval of the track fence sketched in gray.

Near the track I turned left and eased the car along toward the main house, which had its back to me. Near it was a small structure, a miniature of the mammoth central stable building. This smaller version was the family stable, which, in Mr. Jewett's time, had held his and his wife's pleasure horses plus three or four amiable mounts kept for houseguests. Now only Toby and an ancient pony lived there.

On a grassy level spot between the stable and the lane leading to the track, I pulled the VW around in a tight circle and parked it close to the flank of the stable. I left it pointing toward the lane and pocketed the key. My heart was thudding.

After easing the car door open, I stepped out and let the door close gently, just far enough to extinguish the ceiling light.

Suddenly there was a snarl, a rush of movement.

The dog hesitated a few yards away, head down, hackles up.

"Casper," I whispered, "it's me, Gusty. Come here."

He collapsed into welcome and came to shove his head under my hand.

"Quiet," I whispered.

This time I had come prepared. In my hand was a small plastic flashlight I'd bought at an all-night convenience store across the highway from the

Holiday Inn. I didn't turn it on until I was inside the stable with the door rolled shut behind me.

Horse and pony shuffled and whuffled at my intrusion.

"It's okay, it's only me." I tried to make my voice normal, to reassure them, while at the same time keeping the volume down as far as possible. At this time of night there shouldn't be anyone awake and about, but . . .

I was thankful for the unlocked stable door, although I had expected it. Most of the stables on the place were left unlocked at night in case of fire, when horses would have to be released without delay. Only the stud barn, with its ultravaluable residents, was locked at night. The main entrance gates were kept locked at night, I knew, but the back road via the track area was considered too remote from the main buildings to be a threat to security. No one, driving along the public road, would know where that anonymous little field access led.

Safely inside, I switched on the flashlight and aimed it toward the ground. This stable wasn't one of my usual haunts, but it was a pretty standard little stable: center aisle; four box stalls along one side; on the other side, two stalls, a tack room, and a feed and tool alcove.

I looked down the row of four stalls. The first was empty. The second held the elderly pony, who blinked at me but hip-sagged back into sleep position immediately.

In the third stall Toby stood looking down at me from his impressive height, his eyes gleaming wet in the dim reflection of the flashlight.

He moved uneasily away from me as I slipped

through the stall door. He disliked either the flash-light or the hour.

"It's okay, Toby. Mutt. Easy, old boy." I rested my hand on his back, stroking, stroking, working up toward his neck, his halter. Under my touch he quieted and stood.

My fingers wrapped around the leather halter under his chin. He jerked lightly away, disliking my hand that close to his sensitive mouth.

You poor thing, I thought. What did they do to you?

Gently I brought his head down and toward me, playing the beam of the flashlight against his neck, working it gradually, gradually toward his eye.

With the beam at last fully on his left eye, I could see that it was clear. A dark brown circle of eyeball, purple racetrack-shaped iris contracting from the light.

No white spot.

It was the other eye then. I eased around his head, switching the flashlight to my other hand, and once again began the beam's approach, up his neck, past halter ring at the base of his ear, and, finally, dead on the blinking eye.

The blinking clear brown eye . . . with no white spot.

12

I was so nonplussed by the collapse of my theory that I stood there for several seconds, trying to sort it out, before I remembered where I was.

I left the stall, crept back down the aisle, and rolled open the outside door.

There was a flash of movement, a grunting sound, and a crashing, ringing blow to the side of my head. Lights popped behind my eyes, and ears ringing, I slithered down a long black tunnel.

I woke by gradual stages. My head was a balloon filled with pain, and my eye, the one that would open, showed me only gray-brown blurs. As sensation began to return to the rest of me, I felt a softly gritty surface under my right side and something hard against my left foot. Somewhere not too far from my face, Casper snuffled.

I tried to lift my head, to sit up, and immediately wished I hadn't. What vision I had began to swim, and the bells rang again inside my skull.

My arms began aching. They were pulled behind me uncomfortably, and they wouldn't come forward.

Things began to clear a little then, and I was able to lift my head far enough out of the sawdust—sawdust?—that the lower eye could be opened.

114

Working as a team once again, my eyes cleared and focused, and I could see where I was.

I was in a rough-planked chute or narrow stall of some kind, about three feet wide by maybe six feet long, with sawdust on the floor and spaces between the boards up beyond my line of vision.

With a flopping twist I managed to sit up. My hands were tied behind my back, making my arm and shoulder muscles ache almost unbearably, but at least my head was clearing a little.

As the ear ringing died away, I became aware of voices beyond the plank partition, no more than a few yards from where I sat. Two voices, both male, both familiar. If I could just get my wits together enough to concentrate . . .

Working my stiff neck, I looked around and up. Up showed me something interesting. A glassed skylight almost directly overhead, but far up. The stars beyond it belonged to another universe.

Skylight. Of course. I was in the square stone breeding shed, and this chute thing would have to be the enclosure in which the month-old foals were held safely out of the way while their mothers were being bred.

Knowing where I was didn't really help, though. I leaned forward and tried to concentrate on the voices.

"I know that, stupid. If you got any better suggestions . . ."

"Let her go. What can she . . ."

The voices raised and lowered maddeningly, so that I caught only snatches.

". . . she's a kid. Nobody's going to listen to anything . . ."

". . . take chances! I told you that a long time ago . . ."

"Well, she couldn't have told anybody anything. She don't know nothing! If you hadn't started bashing her on the head, you ignorant . . ."

"If we leave her alive, we're cooked. I'm telling you. We got no choice. She'll report it, if she hasn't already, and you and I are going to be doing hard time for a lot of years."

"Yes, and if we kill her, it'll be a lot more years or the chair."

"Listen, R.B., we've got our asses in a sling here, and there's only one way to get them out. Get a grip on your guts, and let's get it over with. I can get rid of the body. That's no big deal. We just have to *do* it."

My flesh froze.

I twisted my hands, struggling against the ropes, knowing it would do no good. The shed was locked. Randy and R.B. were sitting between me and the door and would surely be on me before I could get to the door and get out, even if my hands were free and I knew how to open the lock. And that door was the only possibility. No other doors, no windows except the skylight, and it was twenty feet above, with no access to it at all, no beams, nothing.

I glanced through the planks of the chute toward Casper. He had stretched out in the sawdust and begun licking his forepaw, where grass eczema caused itching in the summertime. I glared at him. If he'd been any kind of a guard dog—but of course, from his viewpoint, this was just a pleasant evening's diversion with people he knew.

I thought about trying to coax him into the chute, getting him to chew through or pull loose the ropes around my wrists. Snorting silently, I admitted the impossibility of that. He'd have no idea what I wanted him to do.

I tried to collapse my spine so that I could pull my arms forward, under my butt, pull my legs through, and at least have the comfort of getting my arms in front of my body.

Wouldn't work. Too much body, not enough arms.

I turned my attention again toward R.B. and Randy, who were easily recognizable when I leaned forward and pressed my nose against the splintery plank so that I could see between the boards. They were sitting cross-legged on the sawdusty floor, with my flashlight lying between them. The beam was aimed at the blank far wall, but enough light was shed along the way to show Randy's long blond waves, and R. B. Bates's beak-nosed profile.

They were young, like me. They were not overly bright, either one of them, but they were cornered— and they were dangerous.

They could kill me. They might very well do it. I fought the panic that made me want to yell and get their attention.

Yell?

Would yelling bring anyone else? Jackson Johnson maybe? His apartment was over the stud barn, not thirty yards from here. He was little and old, but he was my friend.

Would a yell carry through these stone walls? Could it possibly bring help fast enough, because as soon as I started, R.B. and Randy were going to be all over me.

And would I even be able to? This all felt so

much like a dream, the kind of dream in which you try and try to scream, and nothing comes out.

Randy said, "The longer we wait, the worse it'll be. We have to do it and we have to do it now, before she comes to."

That did it. I threw back my head and screeched. The word *help* was in the screech, but it was mostly just pure volume, as loud and as shrill as I could make it. No stopping for breath, just screams one after the other.

Casper leaped to his feet, barking foolishly.

I heard the men scrambling up, too, coming toward me. Desperately I screamed on.

They plunged into the chute, grabbing me, pulling me up, clamping a bitter-tasting hand over my mouth. I bit the pad of flesh that was against my teeth and yelled again.

Abruptly the room was flooded with light. Twisting away from Randy, who held me, I could see the open door and my blessed savior, Jackson Johnson, standing in it, his hand still on the light switch. He was wearing only a T-shirt and wildly colored boxer shorts above his knobby legs and boots. I laughed in a flood of relief.

But the boys weren't acting right. They weren't letting go.

"What's going on here?" Jackson asked. Naturally. What else would he say?

Randy answered. "We had to take her, Uncle Jack. She found out about the horses. She was in snooping around Toby."

Uncle Jack? *Uncle Jack?*

The hand released my mouth, and my jaw dropped in astonishment.

Jackson Johnson, my sweet little Popeye guy? My

lifelong friend? Jackson Johnson was the master-mind behind all this? No. Nah, it couldn't be, surely, no.

He was coming toward me now, a ridiculous figure with his boxer shorts and white, hairless, veiny legs, his leathery face a contrast in every way.

He looked at me somberly. "Gusty, Gusty." He shook his head sadly.

"Hey, come on, Jackson," I said, trying for a smile. "What is this anyhow? These guys hit me over the head and tied me up in here. Tell them to turn me loose, will you? My arms are killing me."

"Why did you have to go poking into things, honey?" he asked sadly. "It wasn't ever supposed to hurt anybody. It wasn't."

The genuine pain in his voice came through even my intense worry about myself.

"Jackson," I whispered, "they want to kill me."

Slowly the little man turned and looked from Randy to R.B. and said, "This is it, fellows. No more."

I wasn't sure what he meant by "This is it."

Neither did the boys. They hesitated, glanced at each other.

Jackson said, more firmly this time, "Turn her loose. Just let her leave. If she tells anybody, then she tells. I'm sick of it. It's gone on too long, and now it's hurting people. Good people."

I thought of Pop.

Randy said, "Oh, no, Uncle Jack. You don't just jump off in the middle of something like this. This is our skins you're talking about, me and R.B. We ain't going to prison just because you go soft. Accidents have happened before, they can happen again."

Another look flashed between Randy and R.B., and suddenly they released me and lunged toward Jackson. I fell backward, hitting the back of my head another ringing blow on the corner of the foal chute, so I didn't see exactly what happened next, only that the two of them were on top of Jackson and he was crumpling.

Frantically I scrambled to my feet and made for the door. Running was almost impossible, I found, with my arms behind my back, my body weak and uncoordinated, and the deep sawdust dragging at my shoes.

"Get her," one of the boys grunted.

I plunged toward the door, knowing I'd have to back up to it and grope awkwardly for the handle.

Someone tackled me, hitting me in the middle of my back. I went down, horribly unable to protect my face and chest from collision with the ground.

The crash knocked the wind from my lungs. Craning my head backward, to get my face out of the sawdust, I fought for enough air to get my breathing going again. Bits of sawdust were sucked up into my nostrils. Furiously I snorted them out and opened my mouth, gasping for air.

The weight was still on my back.

I opened my eyes and saw . . . a very expensive ladies' shoe.

13

Mrs. Jewett said, predictably, "What's going on here?"

Friend or foe, I wondered grimly.

The weight rolled off my back, and I was able to sit up and see, in the open door beyond Mrs. Jewett, men. One was a stranger in a business suit. The other two wore beautiful, wonderful, gorgeous police uniforms.

Weakness washed over me with the knowledge that I was finally safe. The nightmare was, somehow, over now. I wavered in my sitting position like a weed in water, and told myself, "No, you are not going to pass out."

Then a blue, pinstriped vest was against the side of my face. Warmth radiated from the solid form of the man who knelt beside me, reaching around me. I sagged against him, neither knowing nor needing to know who he was.

With a series of fumbling small jerks my wrists came loose. Ahhh . . . But my arm muscles screamed and cramped when I tried to move them forward.

The man rubbed my arms briskly, massaging the muscles and flexing the arms and chafing the hands and wrists until life came tingling back. There was movement going on around us, handcuffs being

121

snapped shut, Mrs. Jewett pacing and waving her arms and demanding to know what was going on here. But all I knew was the incredible ached-for tenderness of the man in the blue pinstripes. I wrapped my tingling arms around him and buried my face against his chest and wept.

He lowered his tidy body into the sawdust beside me and held me and rocked me and didn't say anything. I loved him.

In a few minutes I was aware of the party sorting itself out, Randy and R.B., in handcuffs, shuttled into the police car outside, Mrs. Jewett and Jackson Johnson agreeing to follow in Mrs. J.'s Mercedes.

My man said, "I'm taking Miss McCaw to the hospital. She's had some head injuries here. They'll want to watch her, overnight anyway, for concussion. I'll come over to the station after I've settled her in."

He stood me up and brushed me off and half carried me out into the night to a dark anonymous-looking sedan.

When we were on the road, I turned and looked at him. He looked about forty, squarely built, with black hair growing low on his forehead, a huge nose, full, flat-planed lips.

"Who are you anyway?" I said.

"Theo Penn. You called me this afternoon, remember?"

I stared. "You? The Jockey Club guy?"

"Me, the Jockey Club guy." His chuckle came straight from the belly.

"I thought—I didn't think you even took me seriously. You sounded like, when you found out how old I was . . ."

He glanced at me, one eyebrow rising. He had

thick brows, rounded up like the kind you'd carve on a pumpkin. "Oh, I took you seriously. We'd had some complaints about a Tradition Farm horse, Snowball in Hell, I believe his name was. So when you mentioned Tradition, you got my attention. But then you got snitty and hung up on me. And when I tried to call you back, you were gone."

I hung my head, embarrassed. "I tried to call you back, too," I said. "I was just so strung out about what was going on I wasn't thinking very straight. Sorry about that."

He grunted and asked me where the nearest hospital was.

I told him, then said, "I don't need a hospital. I feel okay now." I felt weak and sick, and my head was a bag of pain; but I didn't think it was anything that needed a hospital. He insisted, though, and I was too feeble to fight him. It felt incredibly good to have someone making my decisions for me.

"But how did you get here?" I asked. We were at the edge of town now. "Turn left at the stoplight."

"Well, after you called and hung up on me, I checked a few records, dates and offspring track records and pedigrees and so forth. What you told me seemed to hold up. I kept trying to get you on the phone, and then I got a little concerned. You'd apparently uncovered a wasp's nest up here, and I thought you might get into a bad situation if you went on poking at the nest."

"Which I did," I said ruefully.

"Which you did. So I drove on up here, checked at the motel and couldn't find you, got worried for fear you might have come back out to Tradition on just the sort of foolhardy errand you did come on and gotten your tail in a crack. If they were already following you and were alerted to the fact that you were a threat to them, then coming out to Tradition Farm would be walking right into trouble.''

''So you got some policemen to come with you?''

''Just in case.'' He nodded.

We pulled into the admission entrance of the little one-story hospital where I had celebrated several riding injuries. Mr. Penn handled all the official stuff, and within minutes I was undressed, examined, tied into a hospital gown, sedated, and drifting away.

''We'll talk tomorrow,'' Theo Penn said, leaning over me so my wandering gaze could focus on him.

''I'm very happy to meet you,'' I said, grinning a wavery smile.

''Me, too.'' He touched the tip of my nose with his finger and disappeared.

It was midmorning when I awoke, and two unexpected but welcome faces were looking down at me: Chris and Bobby. They seemed so out of place, so much a part of the confused dreams I'd been having, that it took a minute for me to absorb the fact of them standing there in my hospital room.

''What are you guys doing here?'' I croaked. The voice wasn't working very well yet.

Chris grinned down at me in a matter-of-fact way and said, ''We drove up first thing this morning to pick up American Express. Back from the dead, thanks to you. Those are from Bobby and me.'' She pointed to a mass of carnations on the window ledge.

I grinned, tried to sit up a little, winced, and sank back. ''How am I?''

"You're in good shape, considering," Chris said. "I checked with the nurse, and she said mild concussion, nothing to worry about, bruises and lacerations and rope burns. She was dying of curiosity. We all are."

Bobby shuffled forward and looked down at me as though I were some romantic dying heroine. He was so sweet. I wanted to hug him, and Chris, and everybody. The nightmares were over. A melting happiness rippled through me, along with the awakening aches and pains. But they didn't matter anymore. I had friends here.

"You pulled off a miracle for us, Gusty," Chris said. "You have no idea how much getting Mutt back means to Wood Hill."

I waved her words away, and for a minute we just grinned, the three of us. Then they left, and I dozed again.

Theo Penn and Mrs. Jewett arrived to fetch me, but since the doctor hadn't yet appeared to okay my release, we three sat in the room, talking and waiting. It was a double room, but the bed beyond the sheet partition was empty, so we had privacy. Mrs. Jewett arranged herself on the one chair; Mr. Penn and I sat side by side on the bed.

"Okay," I said, "catch me up. What's been going on?"

Theo took in a long breath and said, "Well, you had it pretty well pegged when you called me last night. They're holding Mr. Johnson and the two boys in the county jail while formal charges are being filed. You'll have to give testimony when the time comes."

I nodded, then shook my head. "Jackson Johnson. I just can't believe that." To Mrs. Jewett I said,

"Why? Has he told anyone why he did it? And what did he do, exactly?"

Beneath the carefully applied makeup, Mrs. Jewett's face showed the damages of a sleepless night. Her diamond-crusted fingers laced around her knee. Her expensively booted foot swung in small nervous motions.

"The poor man is confessing left and right," she said. "Apparently the switching of the stallions was his idea right from the first. I still can't believe I've been jogging around the countryside on American Express all these years. Poor Norman was so surprised when I told him. He'd bought Toby for me on Jackson's recommendation, never dreaming. . . ."

Then I remembered something. "The spot on his eye. He didn't have a spot on his eye."

Theo and Mrs. J. looked puzzled.

"Bobby, the groom at Wood Hill who took care of American Express, told me he had a white spot on one eye from a twig injury. That was what I came back to look for last night. I thought if I could identify him for sure, you'd take me seriously." I looked at Theo Penn. "But Toby didn't have the spot," I said, confused.

"Oh, he used to," Mrs. Jewett said. "I remember that now. When Norman first brought him, I remember looking at that little spot on his eye and asking whether he could see all right. Norman assured me he could, said it was just a . . . well, I can't remember now what he called it. Something about white blood cells gathering at an injury site. He said those spots can last for years sometimes and then just fade away. Toby's must have."

We sat silently for a moment. Then I said, "But why did Jackson do it in the first place? And how?"

Theo said, "He won't tell us why. He just says that he was at Wood Hill once, taking some things down for his nephew Randy after Randy went down there to work. He saw American Express, noticed the resemblance between him and Ambassador, heard all the stable brag about American Express's first colts' speed on the track, and . . . took it from there.

"Randy took American Express off through the woods by some back road to an abandoned farm, left him there overnight while he went back, started the fire in some loose hay in the stud barn, got the other stallions out, and played hero getting them back again and putting out the fire. Then he went by a borrowed truck and trailer the next day, around by the road to the abandoned farm, and collected American Express. Then Randy took him to a not-too-honest vet he'd made arrangements with, up by Cincinnati, and had the tattoo removed. Apparently the vet screwed up the job in some way and did some permanent nerve damage that left the poor horse with an ouchy mouth."

"Poor old Toby," Mrs. Jewett mourned.

I said, "And then he took the horse to his parents' farm and left him there until . . ."

"Till Trigger died of colic," Mrs. J. put in. "I asked Jackson about that, and he said the colic was genuine, but if it hadn't happened when it did, he was planning to slip Trigger some bad feed and bring on an attack. He knew Trigger was subject to colic, and at his age a serious attack could easily finish him off or at least make it practical to replace him."

"And when Trigger did get sick, Jackson was on the spot with a suggestion to Norman about a good replacement horse, over at his niece's place. What about R.B.?" I asked. "Where did he come in on it?"

Theo said, "He had to know about the stallion switch because he was assisting with the breedings. He was also apparently blackmailing poor old Jackson out of a hefty part of the man's salary all this time for his silence. And the nephew, Randy. Jackson paid him five hundred dollars to engineer the switch and the fire, and then the boy proceeded to extort small, steady sums from the old guy. Several thousand all told, through the years."

"The health club fund," I said. "Poor Jackson. With those two leeches bleeding him dry, he must have been having a terrible time all these years."

Mrs. J. said, "Well, I think it got out of hand. No one could have known the horse would sire a Derby winner and become such a spotlighted stud. In the normal course of events the farm would have had a nice increase in income from producing some moderately successful stakes winners, we'd have paid off the debts and lived happily ever after, and the whole thing would have blown over. It was just the fact that Ambassador became such a high-priced stud that encouraged those boys to hang on to their jobs and their extortions. Naturally Jackson was getting a percentage of the stud fees, as stud manager. He'd have been quite well off by now if those two leeches hadn't been draining him of every cent."

I pondered for a while, then said, "Debts? You?"

"Oh, yes." She laughed gently. "When my husband died and the estate was settled, there were sizable gambling debts that I hadn't known about. Oh, I had enough to live on, but most of the horses would have had to go. And most of the staff.''

"Was that why he did it?" I wondered aloud. "Just to keep his job?"

We looked at one another and shrugged. It didn't make sense to me. A man like Jackson could have moved to another stable easily. Stable employees were a fluid population, I knew. And I knew that what she'd said just now was true: Neither R.B. nor Randy would probably have stayed so long in his present job under ordinary circumstances. They weren't the types.

"Poor Mary Jean," I said suddenly. "R.B.'s fiancée."

"Bride," Mrs. J. said ruefully. "They were married last weekend, poor girl. And incidentally, there was something about your being fired because some money was found in your apartment? I'm not sure I understood all of that part, but R.B. put that money there himself. Then he told Norman he'd seen it when he was in the apartment looking at window curtains or some such thing. Norman didn't want to believe him, of course. You'd always been such a favorite of everybody on the place. But Jackson supported R.B.'s claim, and no one would think to question Jackson's honesty. At least . . .''

At least not until now. I could read her sad thoughts on her face. I had a sudden urge to comfort her.

The doctor came then and gave me his little talk about getting into a more ladylike profession. He gave me the same talk about every riding injury. We got me checked out and then stood in the hospital parking lot, me holding the carnations from Chris and Bobby.

"What now?" I asked of whoever might have an answer.

Mrs. J. said, "You come back to Tradition, Gusty, dear. You should never have been fired. It's your home for as long as you want it, although I can't say how long the stable will be in operation."

I stared at her.

She said, "Well, dear, Toby has gone back to Wood Hill where he belongs. We still have Attaché, of course, and the mares and young stock, but Ambassador . . ."

Her voice broke, and I realized for the first time what this was doing to her. Ambassador, the pride of her life, was exposed as a fraud. His son Attaché, the other pride of her life, was sired by a horse she had no right to. Her trusted employees were turning into crooks before her eyes, and even her beloved pet horse was taken away from her. No wonder she was having second thoughts about going on with the stable. And there would be the notoriety when the story got out, and the mess of straightening out pedigrees and registrations on all the American Express/Ambassador colts.

The humiliation before her friends in the racing world.

I looked up at her, awestruck at the damage I had done to her. "I'm so sorry," I whispered.

The quality of the woman broke through as her smile broke through her makeup.

"There's nothing for you to be sorry for, dear. Just the opposite. This mess had to be straightened out, and without you it might not have been. So, the apartment is yours again if you want it. R.B.'s little wife was leaving this morning, moving back to her parents as I understand it.''

Theo shifted his armload of flowers and opened the back door of his car to deposit them inside. "I'll drive you wherever you need to go,'' he said.

I gathered my thoughts. "To the jail first. I have to talk to Jackson. And then back to Cincinnati to the motel to check out and get my stuff and my car. Is that too much driving around?''

"Not at all. Hop in.''

Mrs. Jewett gave me a hug, and I returned it, hard, and waved good-bye.

14

We sat at a scarred wooden table in the visiting room, Jackson and Theo and I, with a uniformed guard hovering at the door. I was glad to see Jackson had been given time to get his pants last night, before they brought him in.

He looked shriveled. He'd always looked small and dried and tough, but now he was an empty husk of the man he'd been. Or maybe it was the surroundings that made him seem that way.

I went on with my probe. "But I still don't understand why you did it. It's important to me, Jackson. I've been hurt by this, don't forget. I lost my pop, somehow or other, because of this, and I think you owe me an honest explanation. And don't give me another chorus of that garbage about helping the stable financially. It had to be more than that. I know you."

He looked at me for a long time, as though he were deciding something.

"You're right, Gusty. I do owe you. God knows I didn't mean for your pop to get mixed up in it, or you either. It was okay before he got transferred to the stud barn. It was just R.B. and me that had anything to do with handling Ambassador's breedings. I put the word out that he was temperamental, wouldn't breed in the daytime with all the distractions around. Wouldn't breed with strangers in the building. That was so mare owners wouldn't ask to witness the breedings like they do sometimes. But then with your dad there . . ."

"What did you do to him?" I asked. My voice dropped an octave.

"Nothing, Gusty, honest. It was R.B. He told me later. I yelled at him, Gusty. I told him it was a rotten thing to do, putting vodka in your pop's Seven-Up, knowing he was an alcoholic and wouldn't be able to stop drinking once that vodka hit his system. R.B. just set up the thing, spiked the Seven-Up, gave it to your pop, left him in that office with the liquor bottles there in plain sight. That was all he did, though, Gusty. I swear to that. The accident *was* just an accident, him falling and knocking himself out on that heater and the gas bottle breaking loose like it did. All R.B. wanted to do was just get him drinking again so he'd get fired or at least so nobody'd believe anything he might say about those night breedings. That's the honest truth, Gusty, I'd swear it on my mother's head."

And it was true. I felt it. More gently now I probed again. "You haven't told me why, Jackson."

His face sagged. His eyes held mine. "I loved her."

I sat stunned.

"I know that sounds foolish to a young girl like you. You haven't lived long enough to know what a fool love can make out of a man, especially when he can't show it in the usual ways.

"When she first came to Tradition, when the old man married her, you'd never have known her, Gusty. She was such a fish out of water. He'd met her in Vegas, got drunk, and married her three days

133

later. She'd been working there only a few weeks, cashiering at one of the casinos. But she was wet behind the ears. Lived on a back-roads ranch somewhere, had a husband that got himself killed in a tractor accident while she was still young and pretty, so she went to Vegas for a little change of pace, see. But she wasn't really the type. Why she married Mr. J. I don't know, maybe for his money or just for someone to look after her.

"But when she came here, she was so scared of all his rich friends. She'd come down to the stable and talk to me, hours on end sometimes, when he was off on one of his business trips. She said I was like her daddy back home. She felt comfortable with me. And she loved the horses. Didn't know nothing about racehorses, but she'd pet their noses and talk to them and go off riding on that Trigger horse he bought for her."

Jackson's mind wandered. I waited a few minutes for him to see the memories behind his eyes, and then I prodded again. "So you fell in love with her? Was she in love with you, too?"

"Oh, hell, no," he said abruptly. "She never knew nothing about how I felt. I would never have bothered her with it. And after a while she started, I don't know, growing into her new place, I guess. Started getting her hair done some expensive place, wearing all them rings and bracelets he was always buying her. Started feeling more at home with his friends, I reckon. After that she didn't hang around with the stable help anymore."

The room was silent. Jackson pulled in a long breath and said, "Course, after the old man died, I knew the place was in shallow water, money-wise. We all knew the old boy was hooked on gambling and the place was mortgaged to the gateposts. There was talk of closing down the stable. I was too old to pull up roots. Tradition was my home, and I couldn't stand the thought of the stable folding and me having to go someplace else. For one thing, I wasn't much for saving my money, and I was scared of not making it till another job came along. And"—his voice dropped—"I didn't want to be where I couldn't see her every day. You know?"

My eyes misted.

He went on. "But it got out of hand, Gus. I never expected to get no Derby winner out of it. That's what messed up the whole deal, that and those boys bleeding me dry. I never counted on that either. All I wanted was for the stable to stay in business and for her to have a better horse than Ambassador was. I hated all them that was laughing at her behind her back for buying him. See, Ambassador was the first horse she bought on her own, after Mr. J. died."

He hesitated, then looked at me, begging me to understand.

"I just didn't want her friends laughing at her," he said simply.

Morning fog swirled around me, hiding all but the nearest panels of track fencing.

Nancy said, "Easy canter once around, and let her out to half speed for the last two furlongs. Watch so she doesn't bend out at the curves."

I nodded and aimed Flatbed Annie onto the track. She was a weedy-bodied filly, light chestnut and small at twenty months, but with promise of later development. She buck-jumped a couple of times under me as we started down the track, and I dug my knees into her withers for support.

135

It was three weeks since my night in the hospital, and I was healed over and back in the saddle, literally and figuratively.

Flatbed Annie carried me through the fog at an easy lope, fighting for her head but remaining manageable until the last turn, when she swerved toward the outside in spite of my best efforts. I let her extend the last two furlongs, loving the surge of her under me and the wet dawn air against my face.

After the workout I walked Annie till no steam rose from her sheet, washed her down at the washstand, gave her to one of the other girls to finish walking, and went back to Nancy for my third ride of the morning.

Life was good, just then, but the goodness had a temporary feel to it. The stable was going to be closed. Decisions had been made. Mrs. Jewett had already moved to the town house in Lexington. The racing string was to complete the season and then be sold at auction along with the mares and young stock. Sealed bids were being accepted for Attaché from investment groups.

These days I spent as much time as possible avoiding long-range plans. I rode my workouts, spent the rest of the day filling in for Jackson and R.B. in the stud barn, and tried to make myself too tired, by night, to lie awake thinking.

I'd have to leave Tradition, of course. Another job in another stable. No problem, now that my reputation was washed clean. Chris wanted me at Wood Hill, and I was tempted to go. But I couldn't decide.

Something was wrong.

I'd been shaken loose from my old self during the past month, and now I didn't seem to fit within my skin any longer. I'd felt intensely alive during those days of danger and questions. I'd been using my "talented and gifted" brain to an extent that it was never used by stable work and exercise riding. The brain muscles had been stretched, and now I didn't think I would ever be content again not using them.

Theo Penn came that afternoon, just as I finished filling the water buckets in the stud barn. I invited him up to the apartment, but on the way we sank to the porch steps of mutual accord and sat there instead.

"Do you know yet where you're going from here?" he asked.

He'd been up to see me three or four times, just checking up on my welfare as far as I could tell. He'd always had an excuse for being in the neighborhood, but today he didn't bother with explanations. Today I had the feeling that he'd come with a purpose.

I shrugged and said, "I could go work at Wood Hill if I want."

"You don't want?"

I shrugged again. "I don't know, Theo. I can't seem to get excited about another stable job. I mean, horses are my life, and I don't want to do anything else, and yet . . ."

He nodded. "You're too intelligent. It can be a burden sometimes."

I looked at him and saw that he did understand me. We grinned.

"Gusty," he said tentatively.

I waited.

"Gusty, would you consider doing something for me, for us?"

"What us?"

"The Jockey Club."

I frowned. "Sure, but what?"

Cautiously he said, "The Jockey Club has a security division, as you know."

"You."

"Me, and lots of others. We could use you."

"What!" I gaped.

"You'd be perfect. You have the look and the background to fit in anywhere as a stable hand, hot walker, exercise rider, whatever. At the same time you have an excellent mind, and you have courage. You'd be taking legitimate stable jobs, but sometimes, if we were hearing rumors, for instance, about suspected problems but couldn't substantiate them, you might be taking jobs in stables where you could be of some help to us. Nothing dangerous," he said hastily, "just an eye and an ear to pick up information we wouldn't have access to otherwise. I've talked it over with my department head, and he's all for it. Now don't decide right away. Think it over."

I sat on that porch most of the afternoon, after Theo had left. I sat, and I thought it over.

If I took the job working for Theo, there would be times when I would be in danger, as I had been at Wood Hill. Genuine danger. Thoroughbred racing was a rich sport, with big-bucks prizes to be won, on and off the track. Big money always drew the hungry, the get-rich dreamers like Randy and the weasels like R.B., and the full-blown organized-crime rough guys. You can't grow up in the racing world and not know that.

And besides the danger, there would be the aloneness. I remembered again the isolation at Wood Hill, the ache of wanting to present my best self to Chris, whom I liked, and to Sherry, whom I didn't, and being unable to. If I went to work for Theo, close friendships were going to be pretty rare in my life. My throat hurt a little, with suppressed tears for Pop and for the familiar warmth of my lifelong acceptance within the Tradition Farm family. There was never going to be that again, not as long as I was living the life Theo suggested.

On the other hand . . .

On the other hand, she had warts. Pop's ghost chuckled in my ear.

On the other hand, it would be a way. It would be a way to have my horse-filled life and at the same time to have the mind-stretching exhilaration of challenge and pride in accomplishments. My accomplishments might even help a little bit in keeping my beloved sport as clean as possible.

I tried to feel noble about that, but it was too impersonal. What I felt instead was the belly-warming glow of Theo Penn's smile as he presented me with my future.

So I have a crush on a father figure. I grinned at myself. What's so bad about that? If old Jackson can pull off what he did for his secret flame, the least I can do is go spying for a few years for mine.

Casper came and brought me a gift, the remains of an incredibly dead mouse. He dropped it at my feet and laid his throat across my boot and sighed.

I'd get up in a minute, I told myself, and go upstairs to the apartment and call Theo, tell him he was on. But for now I just wanted to sit and enjoy the company of the dog—and Pop. I could feel him floating somewhere behind my shoulder, cheering me on.

LYNN HALL grew up in suburbs of Chicago and Des Moines and spent her childhood escaping into the horse books and dog books at the local library. After years of working at such varied jobs as assistant dog trainer, secretary in a juvenile parole office, and ad agency writer, she began to write books, finding the same magic in writing horse stories and dog stories as she did in reading them as a child. Several of her novels, including *The Leaving* and *Uphill All the Way*, were named YASD Best Books for Young Adults, and *The Leaving* also won the *Boston Globe–Horn Book* Award. Her most recent books include *If Winter Comes*, *The Something-Special Horse*, and *Tazo and Me*.

Lynn Hall currently lives in her dream house, a cozy stone cottage full of dogs and with a horse in the backyard, in her favorite part of the world, northeast Iowa.